Gypsy Campfire Stories

by

G. D. JONES

Copyright © 2019

ISBN: 9798668541942

Published by www.publishandprint.co.uk

All rights reserved. No part of this book may be used or reproduced in any manner whatsoever without written permission from the author.

For privacy reasons some of the names and locations in these stories have been changed.

Big thank you to Dave Lewis, my editor / publisher and a special thank you to all the people who shared their stories with me and made this book possible.

Cover design: Gwyn Jones / Dave Lewis

Illustrations: Gwyn Jones

Romani Gypsy **G. D. Jones** was born in Blackburn, England in 1983. After leaving school at the age of eight, with his mother's help he improved his reading and writing skills by reading children's fiction and The Bible.

Being a huge fan of the paranormal he always wanted to write stories of his own. Aged 23, he decided he was going to do just that, although it would take him ten long years until he would complete his first novel 'The Future Assassin'.

He has since gone on to write 'Theory Tales' and 'Extra Terrestrial Wrestlers' - two collections of wonderful sci-fi stories.

When he is not writing fiction he likes to draw, sing and play guitar, as well as making prank videos for his YouTube show 'Crackpot Videos'.

INTRODUCTION

The Romani gypsy community as had a long history with the paranormal. From ghostly apparitions to UFOs it seems every generation has had at least one chilling experience.

It is a well-known fact that gypsies are a very secretive community, yet there are so many great stories rooted in our history that it feels like a crime not to share them with others.

In this book you will hear true stories from gypsy families from all over the country. From strange encounters with ghosts, UFOs, fairies and everything in between. Stories that have gone untold to the outside world until now.

G D Jones

CHAPTER ONE

THE HAUNTED AMBULANCE
STORY BY C H JONES SR

When I was a child, my father bought an old ambulance van. When we were children, my brothers and sisters and I could all sleep in it during our summer travels.

It was mid-1950 and we had settled in for the night along the commons in Llanelli, south Wales. Everything was fine until about 2am in the morning, when we were all awoken by what sounded like people thumping on both side of the van. When we looked out of the window, no one was there, but the pounding noise continued.

After hearing his children's screams for help, my Dad came rushing out of his own caravan to rescue us. He took us out of the old ambulance and let us sleep in his caravan for the night.

My dad sold the ambulance to a friend the very next day and shortly after we set off once more on our summer travels. I was relieved to be leaving as I didn't want to spend another night in that haunted place.

A few days later when we had settled somewhere else,

my dad told me the real reason why he had sold the ambulance. As he came out of his caravan that night, hearing his children's screams for help, he said that he saw the ghostly figures of what looked to be a team of paramedics surrounding the van.

Maybe some years before there had been an accident while the ambulance was rushing to an emergency, killing everyone on board.

THE CROSS IN THE SKY
STORY BY A B JONES

I was about sixteen years old at the time the following incident occurred. It was late March and my niece

Margaret and I were walking along the fell ends in Cumbria, collecting wood for the fire at home. Gunshots echoed out into the quiet evening breeze from the woodlands near by, but there was nothing unusual about that.

The woods were popular for traveling men in the area who went with their dogs and guns to hunt and kill rabbits. We carried on walking and collecting wood when we saw what looked to be an old condemned house up ahead. Dusk was fast approaching and it was only then did I realize just how far we had come from our campsite.

As we slowly walked towards the creepy-looking house, a man who looked to be in his mid forties came past us on his bike. He rode along the path towards the house and disappeared around the side. We carried on walking and collecting wood, not thinking much about it.

As we came nearer to the dilapidated house I happened to look up at the sky. The sun had almost gone down and there was hardly a cloud in the sky, apart from two very dark ones that had strangely formed into the shape of a huge cross.

I told my niece to look up and when she did, she thought the exact same thing as I did. It was a sign from heaven for us not to go any further towards the house. We threw down the wood and ran all the way back to our campsite to tell our parents.

"It was a sign from heaven"

My mother blessed herself when we told her what had happened. She said that it must've been God's way of protecting us from the man on the bike.

We never went to gather firewood again while we were there. A couple of days later we moved to Appleby fair.

THE LONELY ROAD
STORY BY JOEY LOCKE

My uncle was dating a girl from Gloucester. He was living in south Wales at the time and would usually go and see her every other week.

Just after the turn off to Gloucester, there was a long lonely road with no streetlights for about three miles that eventually led to a little village where his girlfriend lived. One dark winter evening my uncle was driving along this stretch of road when he noticed an old man walking slowly along the pavement to his left.

Don't ask me why but he felt compelled to give him a lift. He pulled over and asked him if he needed a ride. The old man gratefully got into his truck and told him that he lived in the farmhouse at the end of the road.

As they drove along, the old man introduced himself as Bob and told my uncle that he often goes for a stroll at this time of evening, just after tea. My uncle dropped him off home and they said their goodbyes.

About two weeks later my uncle was traveling down that same road again while on his way to meet his girlfriend. To his surprise he saw the same old man walking along the pavement. He quickly pulled over and asked him if he needed a ride. The old man obliged and my uncle dropped him off home again.

"He saw an old man walking along the pavement"

This happened a few more times until my uncle was called away to work and didn't get to see his girlfriend for about five weeks. When he finally had time to see her. He found himself traveling down that same dark road again and expected to see Bob on his usual evening stroll. But on this occasion he was nowhere in sight.

My uncle decided to drop by his house to say hello before carrying on to see his girlfriend. When he knocked on the door an old woman answered. She glared at him as he explained that he was a friend of her husband's and that he had sometimes given him a lift home.

The old woman asked him to describe Bob to her and when he did, she asked him when he'd seen her husband last? My uncle told her that it was about a month ago. He was shocked by what she told him next.

She went on to explain that two years previous, Bob was on his way home after his usual evening stroll and had suffered a massive heart attack along the way. He died in the exact spot where my uncle always picked him up from.

THE BRIGHT BALL OF LIGHT
STORY BY BILL JONES

This happened to me when I was about 8-years old. I'd just come home from school and I asked my dad if I could go out and play with my friend who lived at the other side of the campsite.

He said yes but told me to come home in an hour, in time for my tea.

I met my friend by the entrance of the site. We were

playing soldiers for about ten minutes when our attention was drawn to the heavens.

We saw a huge ball of light, moving slowly across the sky. The descending sun was hidden behind the clouds and whatever this thing was it was heading straight for it.

There was a bright flash of light as the strange object disappeared behind the clouds. Our young minds didn't know what to make of it all and we just thought it had something to do with the sun going down.

We carried on playing not thinking much of it until I heard my dad calling for me to come home. I remember crying because I had only been out for twenty minutes when my dad had promised that I could stay out for an hour.

When I got home my dad told me it was half past five and that I'd been out for over an hour. I wouldn't have believed him if I hadn't noticed how dark it was outside. I sat down confused. Then I realized that somehow, after me and my friend had seen the bright ball of light we'd lost an hour of our lives.

I've read similar cases where people have lost track of time after a UFO sighting. Some have gone under hypnosis and later discovered that they were abducted by tall grey aliens or little green men. Maybe one day I will too.

THE RENTED HOUSE
STORY BY A B JONES

My brother had just rented a house in Darwin. We were a close-knit family so it was ideal that the house wasn't that far down the road from where we lived. He had a German Shepherd dog. I don't remember its name because I was about five years old at the time.

But I do remember it being very friendly and loyal. My brother had been running back and forth for most of that day, collecting all of his belongings from his old property and delivering them to his new home.

When he'd finished, he came for his dog that we had been looking after while he got himself organized. Everything was fine until he got to the house. For some reason the dog would not go inside. He soon found himself having to drag it into the house. When he took it into the living room he struggled to shut the door to keep it safely inside while he went to collect the rest of his things from his van.

When he returned, the dog was nowhere in sight. He soon realized that it had jumped out of the window which he had left open earlier that day. For some reason the dog did not want to be in that house and my brother never saw it again from that day.

"The dog wouldn't go in the room"

A couple of months later, my brother discovered from one of the neighbours that the person who rented the house before him was a spiritualist who regularly held séances there and on more than one occasion had been in contact with the dead.

THE HAUNTED TABBET
STORY BY JOHNNY ANDREW LOCKE

I had been married for a couple of years at the time this happened. The wife and I had just bought a Tabbert caravan from London. Our first evening in our new home was perfectly normal. We put our baby daughter in her cot for the night and we settled down in front of the TV before heading off to bed ourselves.

I awoke around 3am in the morning in a cold sweat. The baby was crying so I got up to see what was wrong. When I went to turn on the light, I noticed a shadowy figure stooped down by the door. I rubbed my eyes and thought that they were playing tricks on me.

When I looked again I saw that the shadowy figure was in fact a young boy. He looked about six or seven years old and as far as I could tell in the faint glow of the moon that was shining through the sky light. He was dressed in old-fashioned clothing. Oliver Twist style.

He remained by the door, unmoving, just staring at my child. I tried to turn on the light but for some reason it wouldn't come on. By now I was freaking out. I tried to wake my wife but she just moaned at me in a dream-like state.

I built up the courage to confront the boy. I asked him what he wanted but he just ignored me and continued to stare at my child. I pressed the light again and this time it came on. I looked towards the door to find that the boy had gone. I ran over to my child and saw that she was now sound asleep. Believing that it was just my eyes playing tricks I went back to bed, but I left the light on.

"Its wings were folded across its face"

A few nights later at around the same time, about 3am, I

looked over to my daughter's cot and nearly jumped out of my skin at what I saw. I can only describe it as a very large bat. It was around 4 feet tall. Its wings were folded across its face and they twitched as it stood upright in the corner of my caravan.

I got up and I switched on the light hoping that it would disappear just like the little boy had a few nights before. But it remained visible. I ran over to the cot and grabbed my daughter and took her into our bed.

I gave it a few moments before I dared to look back at the nightmarish creature. When I did, to my relief it was gone. I managed to wake my wife and I told her what I'd seen. She didn't want to spend another night in there so we got our blankets and slept in my mother's big shed for the rest of the night.

We sold the caravan a few days later.

A couple of months down the line, I was browsing on Gumtree when I noticed the same Tabbert caravan up for sale again.

No doubt that the new owners had been paid a visit from the little boy in the old fashioned clothes and the creepy large bat from hell.

THE DOLLS THAT CAME TO LIFE
STORY BY G D JONES

I come from a big family. I'm the youngest of six boys and one girl. Whenever my dad would go somewhere, like visiting my granddad or go fishing, he'd usually take most of my brothers with him, leaving me and my sister for my mam to look after.

For some reason, on this one particular night, I was the only one left behind. After our tea, my mam sat down in front of the TV going through her usual routine of looking through her cookery books and tearing out pages of recipes she fancied, while I was busy with my plastic sword, pretending I was He-Man. We lived in a Portmaster caravan that was quite spacious with a bedroom where me and my brothers slept.

There wasn't really anything creepy about it because it was just a usual boys room with a TV and a VHS player on top of a table and loads of toys and game boards laying around.

I pretended that my mam's broom was Battle Cat as I rode into the bedroom in my pursuit of Skeletor. But what I saw as I came inside the room still haunts me to this day. Two of my Muppet Teddy bears were dancing around on the bed with their backs turned to me. I don't know the names of the characters but it was the green chubby one with glasses and the one that always accompanied him with the big round eyes and mop head that always said, 'Mememe,' whenever it spoke.

They looked like they had no balance as they danced away. I watched in disbelief for about half a minute before they came to a halt and turned around and looked at me in a creepy unhinged way.

I ran out of the bedroom screaming and told my mam that the Muppets had come to life. She didn't believe me and told me that I was imagining things. I convinced her to come into the bedroom with me so that I could show her and when she did both the Muppets where laying lifeless on the bed. She rolled her eyes and told me it was just my active imagination.

When my dad arrived home, I told him what I'd seen and he threw both Muppets in the bin. Nothing out of the ordinary happened again after that night. For many years I believed that somehow the Muppets had come to life that night. But now as an adult I wonder if I caught an invisible presence playing with them as I came into the bedroom? My brothers always did claim that the caravan was haunted by the ghost of a little boy.

THE CALL BACK
STORY BY C H JONES SR

My uncle and his friend were out calling around the houses. They were looking for scrap metal or anything else they could get their hands on to make some easy cash.

As they drove along the road they came to a narrow lane so they thought they'd venture down, just to see where it led. The lane led to the driveway of a big posh house. My uncle got out of the lorry and knocked on the door to see if there was any scrap laying around.

A moment later an old woman opened the door. My uncle described her as just a normal looking person. There was nothing really unusual about her or her husband who was standing right behind her as he asked if there was any scrap metal laying around their property that they wanted taken away?

They said no but asked him if he did house clearances? They said that they were moving soon and they needed a lot of old stuff taking away. My uncle obliged and they welcomed him and his friend inside.

The house was cosy if not a little eccentric as she led

them to each room showing what had to be removed and what she wanted to keep. They came to the spare room upstairs where most of the junk had been stored out of the way. There were cupboards and wardrobes and boxes filled with cups and plates. My uncle rummaged inside one of the boxes and saw an old pocket watch thrown carelessly inside a cup.

Knowing a bit about antiques he quickly discovered the name of a famous watchmaker written on the back. He would've put it up his sleeve there and then if the woman's husband wasn't watching him curiously. He put it back into the cup and pretended not to have realized how valuable it was. He slyly winked at his friend before saying that they could take the lot away for £20 quid, which was a reasonable price in those days.

The old couple agreed but insisted that they come tomorrow to do the job as they were going out that afternoon. My uncle and his friend reluctantly agreed and said that they would be there first thing the next morning. They laughed and rubbed their hands as they drove away. Believing they were about to inherit a fortune.

Around 9am next day my uncle and his friend could hardly contain their excitement as they entered the narrow lane, which seemed a lot more difficult to drive down than it had the day before with overgrown bushes and trees almost blocking the way.

When they finally reached the end they were shocked by what they saw. The big mansion that they'd been inside only the day before was nothing more than an old condemned house with the door and roof missing and all the windows smashed. The only thing that looked to be keeping it together was the thick carpet of ivy crawling up the walls.

They reversed out of the lane believing they had made a wrong turn or something but after about half hour of driving around and retracing their steps they accepted that this was the house they'd visited the day before.

They had no explanation for their strange experience other than this. Either the entire place was haunted or they'd stumbled into some kind of time slip.

WHEN DEATH CALLS
STORY BY A B JONES

It was early March and it had been a cold grey day. After my children came home from school I went through the usual routine of cooking their tea and letting them watch cartoons on the TV before getting them washed and ready for bed.

When evening came and they were all asleep my husband and I settled down in front of the TV before going to bed ourselves.

I was awoken in the middle of the night by the door of our caravan being forced open, even though I made sure I locked it before I went to bed. I sat up and looked towards the door and watched in sheer terror as a tall hooded figure all dressed in white came inside. The only way that I can describe it was that it looked like a member of the Ku Klux Klan only its masked hood wasn't pointed, it was shaped more flat like an envelope. The figure stopped in the doorway.

We just stared at each other while everyone else was asleep. Suddenly it lifted its arm and pointed at me. The overly long sleeve of its cloak hung down low as it said, 'It's not your turn yet!'

It slammed the door shut as it departed.

Next morning when I woke up I told my husband what I'd seen. He laughed and told me not to worry because it was just a bad dream. He dropped the children off at school before heading off to work himself, leaving me alone with my thoughts.

By 11am I was starting to believe that my strange experience was nothing more than a bad dream. That was until I heard the awful news that my sister Mary had passed away in the early hours of the morning.

Me and my sister Mary looked very much alike, people always used to get us confused with each other. I believe that is why the angel of death came to my home first, before hers, and left me with a warning that it wasn't my turn yet.

FIGHT UNTIL THE CRACK OF DAWN
STORY BY OPEY JOE

My granddad and granny were courting for about a year before they ran away together and got married. They had no money and no home and In those days if times were hard it was common for travellers to knock on farmers doors and ask if they could stay in the horse's stable or wherever else was suitable for a night's shelter.

After a little journey on foot, they came across a farmhouse somewhere in Cheshire, they explained their situation to the farmer and he kindly allowed them to sleep in one of the barns for the night.

The wooden barn was dark and damp. It stank of cow manure but it was better than sleeping outside in the cold. They settled down on a bed of straw and fell asleep. It was pitch black when my granddad was awoken by a noise at the other end of the barn, it didn't take him long to realize they were not alone. Suddenly, the shadowy figure of a man came and pounced upon him. My granny screamed as my granddad began to fight whoever the intruder was.

The intruder was strong but my granddad was determined. The fight lasted until dawn and finally came to an end when my granddad got the upper hand. After the intruder escaped, my granddad rested until he was fit enough to leave the farmyard's premises.

You're probably thinking there's nothing supernatural about this story because the intruder could've easily been a homeless man looking for a night's shelter or even a mugger or an escaped lunatic. But you have to understand that my granddad, Bill Jones, was a well-known bare-knuckle fighter. His fights are legendary amongst travellers and are still talked about to this day.

Some people say that no countryman could ever last two minutes with big Bill Jones in a fight, let alone hours. This is why many believe that the intruder my granddad fought until dawn was not human at all. Some have even suggested that it could quite possibly have been the devil himself!

CHAPTER TWO

SUDDEN GALES
STORY BY GD JONES
(My mother told me these stories.)

It was the day before my granddad's funeral and my mother was standing outside with her family as a black limousine brought their beloved father back to his house for the family to spend one last night with him before his burial in the morning.

It was a cloudy day but there was no wind or rain. My mother told me that as soon as the car came into view a strong gale blew all the clothes off of the washing line. Her sister said that it was a sign from their father that he was happy to be home for at least one more night.

A similar thing happened again to my mother many years later when she was walking my brothers' home from school. She only took her eyes off my brother Jim for a second but in that time he somehow managed to run off the pavement and onto the busy main road. My mam was very emotional when she told me what happened next.

She said that a strong gust of wind pushed her forward just in time to save her child from a speeding car. She believed that the sudden gale was the spirit of her older brother Jimmy who had passed away many years before. She said she always felt like he was still with her and protecting her and the children.

WE LIVE AMONG YOU
STORY BY D THOMAS

Near the town of Monmouth there is a long, dark dual carriageway that stretches for over ten miles. One night while traveling to Gloucester on this very road to visit family and friends, my dad's van broke down. It was 1996 and not everyone had mobile phones like they have today. He had to leave it on the side of the road and hitchhike to the nearest telephone box to call for help.

He thumbed for a ride as he walked along the dark road. A few cars speeded past him before a Volvo pulled up next to him and the man driving offered him a lift.

My dad gratefully got inside and thanked the man as he put on his seat belt. The man didn't answer and despite my dad trying hard to make conversation with him as they drove along, he remained silent.

The man looked to be in his mid 40s. He was completely bald and had bulging eyes that were unblinking as he stared at the road ahead.

'You humanoids don't know your place in the world!' said the man, breaking the awkward silence. 'But you will soon! Maybe not in your lifetime but soon.'

The man's voice was deep and flat and my dad was ready to hit him if he was to try anything.

'You look to the sky and worry about being invaded when the truth is you are already invaded! We live among you! This will be our planet long after you are gone! '

My dad wasn't sure whether to laugh or call him insane. But if the man was joking he was seriously doing a good job of keeping a straight face.

Thankfully, he dropped my dad off at the nearest garage and said before driving off. 'Remember we live among you.'

My dad watched as the car disappeared from view and breathed a huge sigh of relief. He thought if that guy wasn't serious he must be having a hell of a laugh to himself right now in the car. Whether he was joking or not he still frightened the life out of my dad.

THE CARD PLAYER
STORY BY OPEY JOE

So many different versions of this story have been passed around throughout the years that it's hard to know who was actually there when it took place. Here is the most common version of this legendary tale.

My granddad Bill Jones was in a pub called the Farmers Arms in Llanelli, south Wales. He was playing cards with his drinking pals Sammy Lee, Jim Price and Addie Lee. It had gone 10pm and they had been drinking, smoking and gambling, playing three-card brag and poker since 7pm.

They had just finished another game when a man dressed in a dark overcoat and trilby hat came to their table.

'Mind if I join you?' he said, showing them a wallet full of notes.

The drinking partners welcomed him to play and so he pulled up a chair and joined in the game.

They went from three-card brag to poker to rummy to pontoon but no matter how hard they tried the stranger could not be beat.

Every time he won a hand he kept encouraging them to up the stakes. When they told him they were running out of money he suggested that they should think about gambling with something else to try and win their money back. My granddad felt uneasy about the man as there was something just not right about his manner and the way he played.

Sammy Lee was dealing the cards when one slipped off the table and onto the floor. Jim Price who was sat across from Sammy Lee and the stranger bent underneath the table to pick the card up. As he reached for it, he was horrified by what he saw. The stranger had a hoofed foot, like that of a goat.

'Jall! We're playing cards with the old Muller!' said Jim Price to his friends as he placed the card back on the table.

"Jall, we're playing cards with the old muller!"

The stranger smiled to himself as they all got up, left the table and ran out of the pub as quickly as they could.

They never played cards for money again after that night and they certainly didn't return to the Farmers Arms where they could easily have lost their souls as well as their money to the stranger with the hoofed foot.

* Jall means run and muller means devil in the Romani gypsy language

SEEING FAIRIES
STORY BY GD JONES AND BILL JONES

Like every other child in the world I was always fascinated with fairies. By the time I was an adult, my fascination with the little people had disappeared completely. I thought that if there really were fairies or elves living amongst us there was nothing magical or strange about them. They were probably just ordinary men and women who people in the olden days labelled as outcasts of society due to their unnatural deformities and small structure.

Maybe they had gone to live in the woods to get away from all the people who looked down on them so they could just live normal lives together. And then of course, many years later, maybe people who encountered them in the woods thought they were magical beings. I presumed that the magic they were noted for was just smoke and mirrors. Maybe anyone who was caught trespassing was given a taste of a few magic mushrooms or whatever other remedies they conjured up to scare any intruders back to the outside world and make sure they didn't come back in a hurry.

I was certain that's where the legend started. It wasn't until I had a strange encounter of my own that my opinion changed. But before I can tell you what happened to me you must first listen to my brother's strange experiences.

FIRST STORY BY BILL JONES

It was summer of 1997. I had just moved to Formby in Liverpool with my parents and my brothers and sister. In no time at all we had made a dozen new friends on the campsite where we planed on staying for the next few months.

I was in my early 20s and all my brothers and most of our friends were teenagers. More often than not we would pass the time away by walking up the village to buy booze or mess up the grass in the huge golf field next to our campsite. We even smashed the windows out of a big greenhouse just up the road.

There was a long narrow country lane that went on for about a mile before leading to our site. There were trees and shrubs on both sides of the lane that blocked out the sky in parts and made the road so dark at night that you could barely see your hand in front of your face.

One night, me and my brother were making our way home along this narrow country lane after leaving our three brothers and a few of our friends up the village. We were about half way down when we heard a scary voice calling out my name. 'Bill... Bill!' It said in a grotesque voice.

Me and my brother Tom weren't even thinking of anything scary before this happened but now we were shit scared. We heard a rustling in the bushes and we both looked in the same direction. In the faint glow of the moon we saw the silhouette of a small man with a pointed hat. He was laughing as he peeped at us from behind a tree.

We ran for our lives and didn't stop until we got home. No one believed us when we told them what we'd seen and heard.

About three years later, after we returned to south Wales and were living on a campsite in Pyle, Bridgend, I was laying in bed unable to sleep. It was a windy night and all of my brothers were sleeping. I was starting to drift off when I heard the door of our caravan blow open.

I immediately put it down to the wind and was about to get up and close it, as my bed was closest to the door. That's when I saw the silhouette of a little man once more. This time he wasn't wearing a hat and he looked completely bald. He pounced on me and put his small hands around my neck. In a much more pleasant voice he said, 'I'm sorry... but I have to do this... I'm sorry...'

With all the strength in my body I managed to overpower him and sit up straight in my bed. I quickly got up and looked around the caravan but the little man was gone.

SECOND STORY BY GD JONES

As soon as I opened my eyes that morning, my brother Bill was telling me about his strange experience. We slept in the same bed only at opposite ends and I told him that if it were true I probably would've heard something. To be honest I didn't really believe him. I put it down to either a bad dream or he was just making the whole thing up.

I got up, had breakfast and went to work. I didn't think about what my brother had told me again for the rest of that day.

Late that night at about 12am I was laying in bed unable to sleep. All my brothers were out for the count and I was thinking about an upcoming WWE Pay-Per-View that I couldn't wait to watch. I wasn't even thinking of anything scary or what my brother had told me earlier that morning when I noticed the silhouette of a small man approaching the bed.

In no time at all he leapt up at me and I was completely paralyzed from head to toe like someone suffering from sleep paralysis.

After a struggle, I managed to lift both my hands and grabbed it around the neck. With all my strength I forced myself to turn over and ram its head into the bed bunk. I clearly had it gripped but I couldn't feel anything in my hands. I kept thrashing its head against the bunk until it disappeared and my strength returned to my body. After this happened I felt exhausted and fell into a deep sleep.

Next morning I told my brother about my experience with the little man and he laughed for not believing him the day before. We told everyone in the family and as expected they didn't believe us either! Everyone apart from my brother Tom that is, who remembered what he'd seen in Formby.

We were drinking tea and talking about our experiences for most of that morning. Then suddenly we both stopped dead in our tracks when we noticed something in the garden.

There was a huge brown toadstool right in the centre of it. Don't ask me why but it was very creepy looking. My brother quickly ran over to it and smashed it to pieces with a stick. When I asked him why he did it, he told me that the little man we saw was a fairy and that the toadstool was probably his portal to get to our world.

He said he saw a similar one down the lane in Formby but didn't think much of it at the time.

We were never visited by the little man again. And we were never quite sure what he wanted or what he meant by saying, 'I'm sorry, I have to do this.' The toadstool has never returned to our garden either.

THE NIGHT I WAS ABDUCTED
STORY BY C H JR

We were living in Salford, greater Manchester at the time this happened. I'd just come back from a night out with a few of my friends from the campsite where we were had settled in Dutchy Road. We had two caravans on the same plot. My parents slept in the one we kept for best with most of my brothers, while I slept in the one we lived in with my other brother and my sister.

Everyone was sleeping when I got home. I was very drunk and despite my best attempts to keep quiet and not to wake anyone up, I tripped and bumped into everything in my path. I did manage to get into bed without waking anyone though. I was exhausted and feeling a little sick but in no time at all I was sound asleep.

I woke up in a strange bright room. I was laying on a round table and I was completely paralyzed. I soon noticed several small figures standing around me. They had thin bodies with big heads, huge black insect eyes and green skin.

I began to struggle with all my might to free myself as they crept closer with surgical like equipment in their hands.

They stopped and stared at each other before I heard one of them speak telepathically to the others.

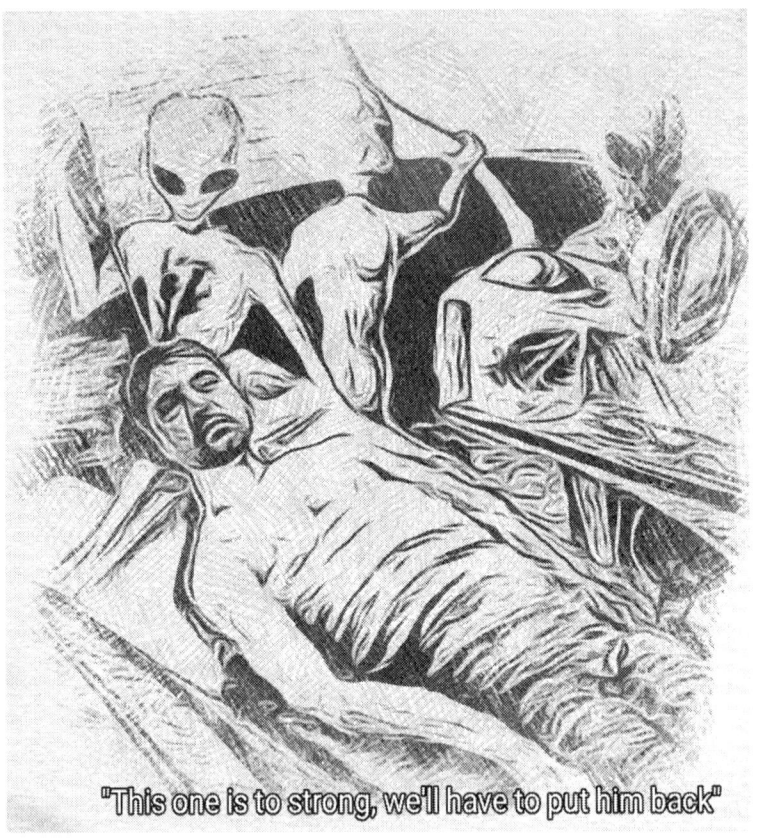

'This one is too strong we will have to put him back!'

It was morning when I woke up and told my family what

had happened. No one believed me accept for my youngest brother Gwyn. My brother Bill, who slept in the same caravan with me, said I dreamt the whole thing up, because he had been watching the movie 'Fire in the Sky' that is about Travis Walton's real life alien abduction.

He said that he fell a sleep while watching it and it must've still been on the TV when I got back.

I don't know how true that was but I couldn't argue the point because I was drunk when I got home that night. All I know is that it felt very real at the time. In later years, I kinda got embarrassed whenever one of my brothers would bring it up in front of someone. I didn't want to be a laughing stock amongst travellers so I started to deny it ever happened. It wasn't until I heard about 'G D JONES'S GYPSY GHOST STORIES' that I decided to contact him and share my experience with you all.

GHOST GLASSES
STORY BY SAMANTHA KNIGHT

When I told G D JONES this story, he said that it could easily be a number one bestseller if I was to novelize it. I think it was a nice way of telling me that he didn't really believe me. To be honest, if someone told me what I'm about to tell you I wouldn't believe them either.

My aunt Rose was a medium. She did a lot of séances in her caravan. She did it for a living.

As a child I was always scared of her. She was quite a large lady with dirty silver hair. She always wore big round glasses with sticky tape holding the frame together. Sometimes she'd come and visit our house and whenever I saw her she always seemed to be looking and talking to someone else next to or beside me. Someone who was invisible to everyone else accept her.

She passed away when I was eighteen years old. My mother and brother were both upset when they got the news but for some reason I wasn't. I just thought she's not actually gone, she's just moved on to a different place.

After the funeral I went over to her caravan with my mam and my little brother. We cleared out everything she had in there. After we'd packed up all her clothes and jewellery along with her endless collection of books on the paranormal, we locked up the caravan and left the campsite where she had lived.

I was awoken in the middle of the night by my brother banging and screaming on the door for me to let him in. I didn't want our mother to be disturbed because she'd had a stressful day so I quickly opened my bedroom door and my brother ran in and locked the door behind him. I turned on the light and told him to calm down. He was only twelve and he was sobbing his heart out.

"Whoever wore the glasses was given special sight"

I asked him what was wrong and through his tears he told me that he'd tried on auntie Rose's glasses and he saw an old man standing over his bed.

As soon he handed me the glasses I knew that he was telling me the truth. I told him he could sleep in with me for the rest of the night and threw the glasses onto the top shelf of wardrobe.

The next day my brother got up and acted as if everything was normal. I didn't want to cause my mam any more stress so I didn't bother to ask him about what he'd seen. We ate our breakfast before my mam went to drop my brother off at school.

While alone in the house, I went to get my auntie's glasses from the top of the wardrobe. I walked into my brother's room and put them on. I could see through the lenses perfectly as I looked all around the room for any signs of the old man. Nothing! Not a trace. I took them off and decided I would try again later.

But I didn't intend to stop there. I always believed that whoever wore the glasses was given some kind of special sight. To see things that were invisible to the ordinary human eye. That's why my auntie was so good at her job. Not because she had powers but because her spectacles did. Where she got them from I shall never know but now they were mine I intended to use them at every opportunity.

I put the glasses on again later that evening while my brother was sleeping and didn't see anyone else inside his room. Anyone else would've put it down to a bad dream but I refused to give in.

Whoever he saw was not there now so whoever it must've been was probably just passing through our house and my brother was lucky enough to catch him.

I wasn't working at the time and a few days later I had an interview in the job centre. As I was walking back I noticed a funeral taking place in the local cemetery.

This was the chance I'd been waiting for to test out my ghost glasses. I walked up to where a group of people gathered around where they were about to lay their loved one to rest.

I blended in quite nicely as I walked closer to the crowd as I'm usually dressed in black. I took a deep breath before putting on the glasses. At first I saw nothing out of the ordinary. Just a few people sobbing and trying to console one another.

Then I saw her. She turned around and stared at me while everyone else was looking down at the hole in the ground where the coffin had been placed. She was all dressed in grey and her hair was white as snow. Her skin was pale and wrinkly and her eyes were as green as the grass. When she smiled at me it was the creepiest thing I have ever seen. It still gives me chills thinking about it.

I immediately took the glasses off and she disappeared. I noticed a picture of an old lady through the window of the hearse. Surrounded by flowered wreaths saying 'Mum' and 'Granny'. It was her! The old lady I'd just seen! Don't ask me why but out of pure curiosity I put the glasses back on and I almost fell backwards when I saw her standing right in front of me. I took off the glasses and ran all the way home.

I threw the glasses on the top shelf of my wardrobe and left them there for a month.

We lived in Bristol at the time and I found work in a local paper shop. One day while chatting away to a customer she happened to bring up a notorious haunted cinema in Union Street.

Union Street wasn't all that far from where we were living at the time so on my next day off I decided to take a bus to visit it.

I remember seeing a black car with blacked out windows parked not that far from the bus stop where I was waiting. It just looked suspicious and out of place. By the time I got on the bus and was a few miles down the road I'd forgotten all about it.

I did a little research on the place and apparently the cinema was haunted by a man called Robert Parrington Jackson. He was the manager of the place at the time he was mysteriously shot in the head and killed. Many people believed that he has haunted the cinema ever since and strangely enough, only appears to women.

I didn't want to raise any suspicions when I arrived so I got a ticket for the nearest film available. The movie was showing on screen four and I took my seat.

The place was empty and while it stayed that way I decided to put on my glasses. I was sat right in the back row, just so I could have a good look around the place.

Straight away I noticed a man sitting alone in the second front seat by the aisle. The lights were still on so I could see clearly as he slowly turned around to look at me.

If this was the guy who'd been shot I wanted to go down and talk to him and ask him a few questions. All that went out of the window however when he got up from his seat and started to float up the stairs towards me.

I'm sorry to say that when it comes to meeting ghosts I'm nowhere near as brave as my auntie Rose. I ripped off my glasses and ran down the stairs blindly. I ran so fast out of the cinema that I tripped on the pavement and nearly chipped my tooth as I fell flat on my face.

The glasses flew out of my hand and landed a few feet away from me. My knee hurt as I got back to my feet. I went to pick my glasses off the floor but I was beaten to it by a man wearing a black hat and matching suit. I think these belong to you he said in an odd voice that I honestly can't describe.

'They are my late auntie's. I'm looking after them now,' I said.

He handed them back to me and told me to put them on and look up at the clear blue sky. He was wearing sunglasses so I couldn't really get a good look at his face but there was something menacing about him and I felt compelled to do what he asked.

I put the glasses back on and looked up into the sky. Up in the air there were hundreds, if not thousands of strange flying objects.

Some were traveling fast through the sky, others were traveling far slower while some stayed in one place, as if they were observing their surroundings.

I took them off and looked back to the man in black.

'There are some things people are not supposed to see. And if they do see them they can land themselves into a hell of a lot trouble,' he said. He held out his hand for me to give him the glasses back and I did so without hesitation.

He smiled at me and said good day before heading back to his car parked across the road. It was the same black car I'd noticed earlier at the bus stop. The car sped off and I ran back to the bus station. I'm pleased to say that I never saw the glasses or the man in black again.

I know this all sounds a little far-fetched and I know most people won't believe me. I don't go around telling everyone this story and because of it I have asked G D JONES to make up a false name for me in this story. When I saw G D JONES'S post on *Facebook* asking for ghost stories from the gypsy community I just had to contact him. Believe me or not it's up to you.

FRIGHT TIPPING
STORY BY HOPE AND WILLIAM

My brother and I are tree surgeons. We spend most of our days cutting down overgrown conifers or tidying overgrown hedges. Its hard work but the money is great.

One evening after finishing work we went to tip in a local farm where we live in a little village called Margam. We had a full vanload and needed it empty to start on another job the next morning. The farmer who owned the place usually stayed opened until around 8pm. He was making so much money from all the travellers in the area that he had to buy a huge shredder to keep the rubbish under control and avoid a visit from the environmental health.

For some reason that evening the farm was closed. We decided to go home and call back later. When we returned at around 7:50pm the farm was still closed and all the lights were out in the house.

There was no guarantee that it would be open the next morning and we really needed the van empty for the next job. We decided to fly tip. It was only conifer trees and not like it was dirty rubbish. We headed for Bridgend.

"it was darker than dark"

We parked up in a dark country lane in Laleston, my brother kept watch while I did the dirty work. The moon was out and my heavy breathing misted the air in front of my face as I pulled branch after branch out of the back of our van and threw them into some bushes. I wasn't thinking about ghosts, I was just hoping a car wouldn't appear down the lane and catch me in the act.

Then something caught my eye in the hedgerow. It looked like the shadow of a giant disfigured man only it looked darker than dark if that makes sense? I stood there frozen, as its shape grew even taller and limped towards me. It said something to me that I couldn't understand. It's voice sounded like a tape playing backwards but in slow motion.

I took off as fast as I could up the lane! I left the van behind not daring to look back. My poor brother Hope, who said that he was already experiencing ghostly chills even before he saw me running past him up the lane, couldn't start the van. The ignition was faulty and sometimes you had to turn the key twenty times before it would start.

I stopped after about half a mile to catch my breath and I heard the van come speeding up the lane. My brother pulled up next to me. He was crying as I jumped inside. I told him what I saw and he said, 'I knew there was something out there... I had a funny feeling we were going to see something.'

We sped away with the back doors still open and trees flying out all over the road. We never fly tipped again after that night.

After that day I told my younger brother what we'd seen and he said that the Laleston lanes in Bridgend are notorious for ghost sightings. He himself had had experiences there. He said that one night while taking a shortcut through the lanes he saw someone crossing the road dangerously. He slowed down and flicked on his lights to full beam and there wasn't anyone there. The scary thing was that there was a cemetery close by and that's where the figure appeared to come from.

Another time he was parked up down some lanes in nearly the same area with his girlfriend. They'd parked up on a verge in the road and were discussing where they should go out for a meal when he saw something walk behind the van through the passenger wing mirror. He waited to see if they would pass through the other wing mirror but nobody did.

He turned to his girlfriend and was about to ask her if she'd made up her mind up about where she wanted to go. But she stared at him curiously and said, 'Did you see that? We're parked up in Pen Y Fai and someone just walked behind your van! Don't you know that just in front of us is a haunted castle and behind those trees there's an old condemned house that's supposed to be haunted?'

My brother sped away as fast as he could. A few years after that he told me what a friend, Bethan Jenkins had seen. Her mam's house wasn't too far away from the condemned house in Pen Y Fai and she'd just returned from travelling. She was home for a week and one night around 12am she said she had an urge to look out of her bedroom window. When she did she saw an old woman standing in the middle of her back garden. She was dressed in a nightgown and she was staring back up at her with her head tilted to one side.

Beth looked away and when she looked back the old woman was gone.

Another strange experience happened to our friends somewhere down those same lanes. There were a few of them in the front of the van. Too many in fact as not one of them wanted to ride in the back after playing pool in a Labour club for hours.

They took a short cut home to Pyle through the lanes and were laughing and joking when they saw what looked to be an old man walking towards them in the middle of the lane.

They slowed the van down and turned down the full beam on the headlights when he disappeared before there eyes.

So many people who have either parked up or passed through the lanes claim to have had a creepy experience like me and my brother experienced. I don't know if some of them are figments of their imaginations but for two men who didn't know anything about the place's creepy history, I can tell you that what we experienced was very real.

THE TALL HOODED FIGURE
BY JIM AND TOM

We were stealing bottles of Calor gas from Steelmans scrap yard in Briton Ferry, south Wales. We lived on spare ground with loads of other travelling families at the time and the scrap yard was over the other side about a quarter of a mile away.

We waited until it was dark before me and my brother Tom sneaked inside Steelmans yard. We broke into his shed and checked the tills. They were empty. We carried on with the plan and took one bottle of gas each from around the side of the office.

There were a couple more we wanted so when we got back we decided to go back for the rest. Mr Steelman liked to stock the bottles up for the gas heater in his office.

We were walking on the pathway back towards Steelmans when we noticed something up ahead. There was a motorway bridge above us so the pathway was lit up with road lights.

There were reeds on either side of the pathway and to the left there was a creepy figure dressed in a dark hooded cloak. It stood in one place, towering above the reeds with its head down and its arms folded. Bare in mind these reeds were about three metres high so this thing must've been over fourteen feet tall!

We both saw it at the same time and both ran all the way home without looking back. We told our mam what we'd seen and she said it was a warning to stay away from that area. She didn't know what we'd been up to so we took her advice and never went back there again.

We told our friend John Locke what we'd seen and he said he'd seen the cloaked figure too in the same place around about the same time at night.

There is an old tower covered in ivy not far from where the hooded figure was sighted. John and his brother Carl believed that, whatever it was it dwelled in there.

DEATH RIDE
STORY BY SHANE OWEN

I was buying a Yorkshire terrier pup from Wolverhampton. The drive from Chester where I lived to the address of the person who was selling the dog was about a two-hour drive. For the cute little puppy that was advertised on Gumtree though, it was definitely worth the trip.

I tapped in the address into my new sat nav that I'd attached to the dashboard of my van. Straight away a ladies voice with an American accent pointed me in the right direction.

Everything was fine until I was about a hundred miles from Wolverhampton. The sat nav directed me to turn off the motorway. I knew this couldn't be right with so far left of the journey so I stopped in the services and re-entered the address.

Then the same thing happened again, the sat nav told me to keep off the motorway and take a different road. This was a pretty modern sat nav at the time when they weren't built into a smartphone. I didn't quite know how these things worked so I thought maybe there were road works on the motorway ahead and it was taking me on a different route for that reason.

Against my better judgment, I followed its directions. It wasn't long before I regretted my decision. There I was driving down the narrowest country lane I had ever been down in my life. The hedgerows at either side of the lane were untamed and were hanging over so much in parts that they were beginning to scrape the paintwork off my new van, while all the time the sat nav advised me to keep going straight.

'In a quarter of a mile, take a sharp left,' said the built-in voice.

The road finally opened up a bit and I saw the turning. *Keep going straight for half a mile*. The lane became narrow again.

I was traveling down slowly in case a car came speeding around the corner when I was forced to slam on my brakes as a fox ran out into the road. It seemed startled and stopped and stared at me for a few seconds before disappearing onto the other side of the hedgerow. How lucky was I to see that fox? Very, I thought, because after it had passed I noticed the road ahead drew right up to the edge of a cliff!

I got out of the van and walked to the very edge of it and looked down. It looked like I'd drove up a mountain. There was about a two hundred foot drop below me.

If the fox hadn't have stopped me in time I probably would've drove straight off! I jumped into my van and reversed all the way back. The sat nav was still telling me to drive forward for another half a mile. I grabbed it off my dashboard and threw it out of the window!

When I reversed out of the turning I saw I sign saying no through road. I was so busy looking at the sat nav that I hadn't noticed it on the way in.

I am a superstitious person and I believe that something wicked possessed the sat nav that day and tried to send me to my death.

Luckily enough though something good was watching over me and sent out the little fox to save my life. I didn't get the puppy afterwards. I was just glad to go home safe and sound.

SPINNING HEAD
STORY BY CHAZZ LEE

I have had so many spooky experiences in my life that GD JONES said he could write a book just about me! Ironically some of the strange things I've witnessed happened to me when I was with some of his brothers. Here is one of them:

It was October 1998. Me and Jim Jones were walking towards the Duck pond in Briton Ferry at around 9pm at night. I'd recently moved to Pyle in Bridgend with my parents. At the time most of my friends, like GD Jones and his brothers, were still on the spare ground in Briton Ferry.

I'd go over to them two or three times a week and we'd either go out somewhere or just hang out and have a chat. Me and Jim were talking about something or other, most probably about girls, when we saw something ahead.

There was a huge motorway bridge going over Briton Ferry and there still is to this day, so the place was pretty lit up with road lights.

First off it looked like a small white terrier dog running around in circles chasing its tail. But as we got closer we could see that it was a human head!

It would spin around and around before stopping for a second before starting to spin again. It made a screaming noise and we both took off home.

I went to visit Jim the next day and we told his mother what we'd seen.

His mam looked at him with a stern expression and said it probably happened because Jim had been wicked to one of their animals. She said that he had kicked their dog that was carrying pups and it died two or three days later.

There are many stories of Briton Ferry being haunted by the travellers who lived there. And I can tell you from experience that it certainly is one of the most haunted places I've ever lived. I have more stories not just about Briton Ferry but about places where I've worked as well.

CHAPTER THREE

THE HAUNTED HOUSES
STORY BY CHAZZ LEE

I met the landlord of a house in Ross-on-Wye. He wanted some junk removing from an old shed in the garden and the two, upstairs bedrooms painted in the house ready for the new tenants to move in.

As soon as I went into the shed I felt a presence, like someone was watching me. The landlord had a dog with him called Mot. It was a friendly little white terrier and it started barking at something as soon as we opened the door of the shed. I had a quick look but soon got out and we headed to the house.

I gave him the estimate of what it would cost to have the shed cleared and the rooms painted. He was happy to go ahead so the following Monday I found myself up the stairs painting the main bedroom. I was working alone as my father in-law, who I usually work with, was out on another job.

I had the radio on loud as I put the first coat of paint on the walls and then went to give my eyes a rest as I'd been working for about an hour.

"The door handle started to turn violently"

I grabbed my phone off the table to ring the wife at home but as I turned the volume of the radio down low I heard something scratching on the other side of the door. I thought the landlord might've come up to the house to check on me and maybe his dog Mot was making the scratching noise.

'Calm down Mot I'm coming,' I stopped when I noticed through the gap under the door that there was nothing on the other side.

Still the scratching persisted.

Then the door handle started to turn violently on itself for a few seconds before just as suddenly coming to a dead stop! Despite being freaked out I turned the radio up full blast and got on with my work.

I managed to paint both rooms that day without further incident but when I finished it was almost dark so I ran down the stairs as fast as I could and got out of there!

Next day I felt the same presence, as if I was being watched, as I cleared out the shed. When the job was complete I went over to the landlord's property to get paid.

I told him what I'd seen and heard while painting the rooms and he didn't seem surprised at all. That's the reason why the last tenants left he told me. They said that, the main bedroom was haunted by an old man. They hadn't had a good night's sleep in the ten months they lived there. They would be awoken late at night by scratching noises on the other side of the door and the door handle turning aggressively. They're five year old daughter told them the old man who lived in the shed wasn't happy about them sleeping in the room where he died.

I'm guessing that the new tenants experienced the very same thing.

HOARSE VOICE
STORY BY CHAZZ LEE

The barking of a dozen dogs echoed out into the quiet morning air until it was drowned out by the noise of my chainsaw as me and my father in-law, Shane, got to work in the front garden of a single terrace house in Carmarthenshire.

The old lady that we were working for was a regular customer and she had a love for dogs. The garden was hard to work inside because it was full of dog litter but we carried on, careful not to tread on or put our hands in it.

The dogs she had would always bark and we got used to hearing them as well as hearing her telling them to be quiet in a deep hoarse voice.

On this one occasion, while we were working at the property, the old lady told us she would be out in the morning and back around lunchtime.

It was around 11 o'clock when we'd finished the job and we were passing the time away at the front garden, smoking and having a chat. We heard the dogs barking like crazy followed by a familiar hoarse voice telling them to be quiet.

After hearing this we assumed the lady had returned home so my father-in-law knocked on the front door. The dogs barked like mad before a hoarse voice told them to shut up. This happened every time my father-in-law knocked on the door yet still no one answered.

We thought she might be busy unpacking her shopping bags so we continued to wait in the front garden.

Not ten minutes went by when a taxi pulled up and out came the lady of the house. We helped her carry the bags into the kitchen while the dogs barked from the living room. She told them to lay down in an angry but clear voice. We told her that we thought we'd heard her shouting at the dogs earlier. She looked at us curiously and asked what the voice sounded like. We said that it sounded deep and hoarse.

She smiled and said, 'Don't worry it's just my late husband.'

Apparently the hoarse voice we'd been hearing all the time we'd worked there was the voice of her dead husband.

FOOTPRINTS
STORY BY JOEY LOCKE

My granddad was calling around the houses with his brothers and his son asking if anyone wanted they're drive tarmacked for a reasonable price.

He came to a shoddy looking house and knocked on the door. An old woman answered with dyed black hair. My granddad said she looked like one of the Adams family, all that was missing was bats flying out from behind her. He got chatting to her and asked her if she wanted the drive tarmacking.

I'd love to but I can't she said, 'The devil is with me and he'll only rip it up!'

My granddad thought she was crazy but still persisted. 'He won't, I'll put it down extra thick so don't worry.'

'I'm telling you he'll rip it up! I've had painters and decorators here, roofers and window cleaners and they've all fell off their ladders!'

After a little bit more persuasion, and a reasonable quotation, she agreed to have it done so that same day my granddad and his brothers and his son got to work. They put the tarmac down and smoothed it over nicely. It was hard work but he was determined to do a good job.

When they'd finished the old woman came out and thanked them for a wonderful job before paying them and throwing in a little tip as a good gesture.

My granddad was living on some old spare ground in his caravan at the time, and after work he and his family would go down to the local pub for a few beers.

They'd just finished they're first pint when the old woman with black hair came in looking for them.

'I TOLD YOU THE DEVIL WAS WITH ME, I TOLD YOU HE'D RIP IT ALL UP!'

'What are you talking about?' said my granddad, trying to calm her down.

'Come to my house and I'll show you!' said the woman.

My granddad and his brothers and his son all jumped into his lorry and followed behind the old woman's car as she led them back to her house. They got out and shined their torch beams onto the drive and couldn't believe their eyes. There were hoof prints leading from the gate right to the front door of the house!

My granddad examined the prints and they were six inches deep.

'Have you had any cows walking down your drive?' he asked.

'Don't be ridiculous! Even if I did the prints wouldn't be that deep, they've even gone through the old concrete base!' said the woman.

My granddad promised her he'd be back in the morning to redo it.

When he went back the next day there was not a mark on the drive. It was just as perfect as he had left it the day before. He freaked out and didn't bother knocking on the door to speak to the old woman. He was so scared that he hooked up his caravan and moved far away from the area that same day.

OUT OF BODY
STORY BY AMY CLARK

I was doing night shifts at a warehouse in Kent. I'm a self-employed gardener but work around Christmas time is always pretty dead so I took on a job as a night watchman.

It was easy work, just sitting around, basically passing the time away on my phone. It was only three days a week and I planned to sleep in the days before work. But that didn't happen. I just could not get to sleep during the day no matter how hard I tried.

After about three weeks my sleep pattern was all over the place. One night, while sitting outside upon an old steel drum, trying to keep myself awake by sipping on a can of *Red Bull*, I dozed off! It was almost daylight when I awoke so I guessed my shift was nearly up. I got up and walked over to the office to make myself a cup of coffee. When I went to open the door my hand went through the handle. I tried several times and the same thing happened.

"I felt like I was being watched"

It was like I was a ghost and I couldn't touch anything. Maybe I'm imagining it because I'm still drowsy I thought to myself. But as I went to turn the door handle, my hand passed straight through it again.

I was in for an even bigger shock when I happened to look back to the steel drum where I'd fallen asleep. There I was still sitting on the drum with my head hung low sound asleep. I looked at myself in a panic and I could see my ghostly body was transparent. I'm dead! Oh God I'm dead! I said to myself.

I thought of my parents and my brother at home and imagined how they were going to react. A sadness came over me as I envisioned them crying.

At that moment I felt like I was being watched. It's hard to explain but for some reason I knew I wasn't alone in that yard. I'm not ready to leave yet I told myself and I ran over to where I was sleeping and flung myself at my own body!

The sound of the morning staff entering woke me up. I got up and checked my hands and the rest of my body. Everything appeared to be back to normal. Some of the staff even said good morning to me.

I have never told anyone about my experience until now. It has never happened again since that day and over the years I have wondered if it was all just a bad dream due to lack of sleep.

All I know for sure is that it was the weirdest experience of my life.

THE GHOSTS IN THE PHOTO AND OTHER GHOSTLY EXPERIENCES
STORY BY CREDDY AND S. S. LEE

Creddy's story

I was about seven years old when me and my family were in the middle of our summer travels with a caravan. We ended up settling on some spare ground in Brighton for a few days. We joined a few of our cousins and friends who had already settled there before we arrived.

One night while me and my dad were gathered around a fire, one of the men stopping there told us that the place was said to be haunted by the ghost of a little boy who had been murdered there many years before.

My cousin had a Polaroid camera and was taking pictures of his wife and their young children that night. It wasn't until the next morning that he called my dad out to look at one of the snaps he'd taken. My dad went milk white as he stared at the photo. Me and my brother tried to look but he wouldn't let us. We moved to another place that same day as my dad didn't want to stay there one more night.

"His face was wicked and twisted"

A few weeks later he told us what he'd seen on the photo. Standing next to my cousin's wife and his children was the ghostly figure of a little boy dressed in old-fashioned clothes. His face was wicked and twisted as he gave the camera an evil stare.

S. S. Lees's story

Me and the wife were having a few drinks at home. As was often the case, by 9pm I'd had one to many. I was making a fool of myself invading the fridge to find food and my wife was laughing while filming me.

Next morning I woke up with a thumping headache. My wife wasted little time showing me the footage of my drunken self on her phone. We were both laughing while watching the video until we saw something unusual at the end.

My wife paused the video and took a screenshot. As I lay on the seat comatose, we noticed creepy faces all around me. One in particular had a beard that you could see clear as daylight. It was hovering right beside me.

This all happened on my father-in-law's yard in Gloucestershire. We were staying there for months and I can honestly tell you it was so dark and creepy on there that I was scared to go out at night to the toilet.

One night my wife woke me up screaming. I asked her what was wrong and she swore that she saw a black shadow hovering over me. I'm glad to say we left there shortly after and never returned.

THREE MISSED CALLS
STORY BY DAWN MARIE

We had just buried my granddad. As all travellers do before the funeral me and my sister and a few of our cousins placed souvenirs in the coffin to be buried with him. I placed the mobile phone he always used to call me on in with him. It was an old Nokia phone that I'd kept in use even after buying a smart phone.

Apart from a few of my customers at work, he was the only one who used to call me on that phone. I figured I'd better leave it with him as I had no more use for it and I could always give my customers my current number.

The morning after the funeral I awoke with the bright morning sunbeams shining through the curtains in my caravan and onto my face. I got up and got dressed. Then I checked my phone and saw that I had three missed calls. They were all timed at 3am. The most horrifying thing about it was that the calls were all from the phone that I had buried with my granddad.

I knew they were from my old phone because I knew the number off by heart. I immediately called it back and to my surprise it began to ring. A few seconds went by before I got an answer.

'Hello,' said a strange deep voice, after a few seconds of silence.

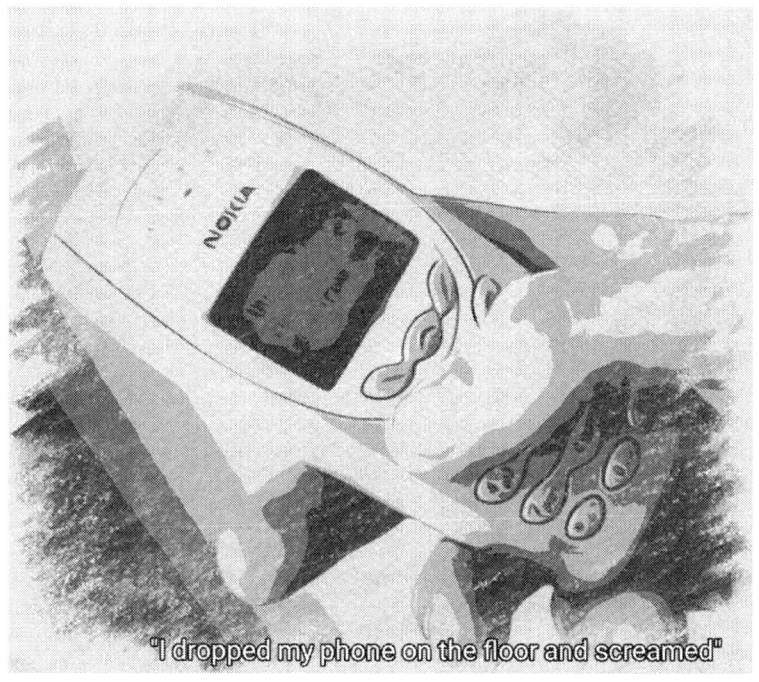

"I dropped my phone on the floor and screamed"

In shock, I dropped my phone on the floor and ran out screaming. I told my parents and my sister what had happened and they followed me back to my caravan. When I picked up the phone it had gone dead. I thought I may have damaged it during the fall and my suspicions turned out to be right.

No matter how hard I tried it wouldn't turn back on. It

wasn't insured so I took it down to a local phone shop to see if it could be fixed.

Strangely enough, when I returned to the shop the next day the guy who worked there said he couldn't find what was wrong with it. He suggested I come back in a few days and when I did I had the same result. The man scratched his head and said he'd never seen a phone he couldn't repair until now.

I ended up getting a new one in its place. I believe that whatever happened when I called that number back, and whoever it was that answered, broke my phone beyond repair.

When I got a new phone the network providers said I could have the same number, even if the SIM was damaged. I started to think that a family member could've pretended to break their phone and do the same thing with my old number, just to scare me as a prank. But everyone I asked swore to me that they wouldn't dream of doing such a thing to me and I believe them.

STRANGE NOISES IN THE WOODS
STORY BY JOEY LOCKE

My Granny and Granddad were traveling about with horse and wagon around south Wales. They set up camp with their tents in waste ground near to some woodlands. As they were putting up the tent they began to hear noises from the woods like trees being blown down with explosions. This strange noise carried on for about ten minutes before stopping completely.

Late that night, while they were sleeping, the noise started again. This time it sounded like people running around their tent shouting and screaming. My granddad Jack wanted to get up to see what was happening but my granny stopped him. Then they both heard what sounded like a car speeding towards them. The noise of a crash followed, as if it had narrowly missed their tent and collided with a tree. Sirens of ambulances and police vehicles filled the air.

In the moonlight they could see the silhouettes of men walking around their tent and trying to rip it apart. They hid themselves under the blankets until the noises disappeared.

Next morning when they left their tent they expected

their surroundings to look like a bomb had gone off. To their surprise, not a tree or a single blade of grass had been touched. They packed up their tent and were soon on their way with the horse and cart.

About five miles down the road they came into a little village and they told the man in the shop what had happened. The man told them that where they stayed was known as the Haunted Quarry.

Your not the first person to have seen something there, the man told them. Every now and then people who have either drove past there or walked through the woods have all experienced the same thing. Nobody knows for sure what happened there but they all have similar stories to the one you have about the place!

My Granny and Granddad never went back there because they believe it was haunted… But I'm not so sure. What do you guys think? Haunted or maybe some sort of time slip?

THE OTHER SIDE
BY TERRENCE CONNOR

I'd just lost my sister. She was only twenty-five years old when she died in an accident. I grieved for a very long time after her death.

One day a friend suggested we pay a visit to a medium called Madam Martha. He said that a friend had visited her and the things she told her were unbelievable.

My granny used to read peoples' fortunes to earn a few quid so I didn't believe in those kind of things and I always thought mediums were just another name for con artist. Anyway, out of curiosity I agreed to go.

When we arrived at the house a skinny old man with a bent back led us to a room where he told to wait for Madam Martha. The room was lit with candles and had all kids of Victorian paintings on the wall. Some of the eyes of the people in the paintings looked like they were staring straight at us.

A moment or two passed before a middle-aged lady came into the room. She had long dark hair and was dressed in black. She sat across from us on the table. There was something about her eyes that freaked me out. They were staring straight at me, unblinking.

'You're sister wants you to know she's at peace!' she said without me saying a word. 'She can't find a way through so she as sent me to contact you. She doesn't want you to be sad anymore. She wants you to get on with your life. You should not blame yourself because it was my choice to go and it was an accident. She said she loves you very much and she will see you again in the next life.'

I sat motionless. I didn't know whether to cry or jump for joy. There was no way she could've known all these things because when we called to make an appointment, we didn't tell her anything but our fake names and fake addresses.

Before I could say anything the woman got up and left the room. When she went through the door me and my friend looked at each other in shock.

'I told you she was good,' said my friend with a smile.

Just then an old woman came into the room. This woman wasn't dressed quite so morbidly, more like a lady you'd see in church. Her hair was grey and she had a friendly face.

'Hello gentleman, sorry to keep you waiting, I am Madam Martha.'

We shook our heads at her and looked puzzled.

'I'm sorry but we thought the other lady we've just seen was Madam Martha?' my friend said.

'Other lady? What other lady? No one else lives here apart from me and my husband.'

We told her what had happened and she looked surprised and said... 'You must've seen a ghost!'

HAUNTED PLACES
STORY BY CHAZZ LEE

I was driving through Kilgetty after going to see my girlfriend. The road to get back to the dual carriageway was long and dark, stretching on for about three miles. The road was said to be haunted by a girl who had been killed crossing over to the other side of the pavement.

I was shit scared driving through so I tried to take my mind off things by turning up the radio.

I was singing along to a song by the band Steps when I happened to look through my wing mirror. I saw legs running at the side of my van, keeping up with me even though I hit my foot on the gas and was doing over 70mph.

I didn't look in my mirror again until I was on the dual carriageway. I haven't gone down that road again since that day.

CREEPY CAR
STORY BY CHAZZ LEE

Another strange experience I had was when I bought a car to get me to work. Every morning I'd drive to work in it I'd notice that something was different inside the car. First it would be small things like the interior mirror twisted around or the seat put all the way back. Other times it would be the radio left on or the lights turned to full beam.

I thought there was some kind of electrical fault with it. One afternoon I stopped by a shop to get fags after coming out of work. Everything was fine when I left the car but when I returned five minutes later the lights were on along with the radio. The driver's seat was pulled right back and the interior mirror was twisted the other way round.

By now I started to think that the car was haunted. I told my mam and sister what was happening and was shocked by what my sister told me.

'I've seen the shadowy figure of a little boy sitting behind you a few times now. The other morning when you were off to work, then again in the afternoon when you were coming home. I didn't want to frighten you so I kept quiet.'

As you can guess I sold the car a day later.

FIVE MINUTES OF FAME
STORY BY RALPH PRICE

When I was young, I always wanted to be famous. The only problem was I wasn't good at anything. I couldn't sing, dance or fight. I wasn't good at sports and I wasn't a funny person.

Still I wanted fame and fortune. By my early twenties it was clear that was never going to happen. I saw other people from the gypsy community who were on TV like

Paddy Doherty and Tyson Fury. I became jealous of their success and I would run them down to anyone who would listen.

I guess it made me feel better about myself. I was still a nobody though and nothing could change that. I left the gypsy site I grew up on to move into a semi detached council house with my wife and two kids. One morning I got up to go to work. I made breakfast and had two cups of coffee to help me prepare for a hard day of block paving.

My wife had gone to stay with her parents for the weekend along with the kids. It was just a regular Monday morning until I opened the door and saw dozens of paparazzi outside my house, blinding me with the flash from their cameras. I ran inside my van and speeded away. I thought someone was playing a joke on me. It would make a good video for YouTube or Facebook.

I stopped at a red light and tried to take in what had just happened. There was a car next to me with a man and woman in the front and a child in the back. The child, who looked about eight or nine, started staring at me. He then thumped his hand against the window and called for his parents to look at me. His parents smiled at me in excitement. They waved and began to call out my name from the driver's window. I speeded off as the lights turned green and they followed behind me, crossing into the right lane even though the car was signalling left.

I eventually managed to escape by turning down a side street. What was going on? How was I famous all of a sudden? How did those people in the car even know my name? To prove I wasn't imagining things I decided to do a test. It was 10am and not far down the road from me was a busy town centre with shops, cafés, bars and everything else. I locked my van and walked gingerly to the town.

What happened when I got there was unbelievable. People swarmed around me, calling out my name and begging for a picture and my autograph. It was terrifying! I'd never experienced anything like it. If this was what it meant to be famous then I'd rather be a nobody any day of the week. I ran back to my van with the legions of fans chasing after me. I literally had to push a few of them out as they climbed into the passenger seat before speeding away.

I had to go back to my house. In a rush to get away from the paparazzi, I'd forgotten to lock the front door. I expected at least a few of them to be waiting for me when I got back but they were all gone. I locked the door and spotted my next-door neighbour weeding the borders of her front garden. I explained what had happened and she said she hadn't seen anything accept me rushing to my van and speeding away. She thought I was late for work.

On my way back to work I noticed the same couple in the car next to me with the child in the back as I stopped at the red light. This time they didn't bat an eye. The lights turned green, they turned left and I went right. Curiosity got the better of me and I ended up parked down the same side street and on my way to the town centre.

This time nobody recognised me. I was a nobody again and I breathed a sigh of relief. I gladly went back to work, a little later than expected. I have no idea how to explain why this happened to me for such a brief period of time but I'm glad to say that it hasn't happened to me since and hopefully it never happens again.

MONKS IN PYLE
STORY BY MANDA LEE

Pyle site in Bridgend is haunted. One of the many things I saw while living there this was one of the scariest.

It was about 11pm at night. The plot where I used to live was right across from the farm field. In the bright moonlight sky I saw a group of monks slowly walking in a straight line across the field. Before they disappeared the monk at the back of the line turned around and looked at me. He stared at me for a few seconds before disappearing with the rest.

NO BAD DREAM
STORY BY HOPE JR

I woke up in the middle of the night one time to discover I was paralysed. I couldn't even call out to my parents for help. I felt a sharp fingernail slowly running across my head and down to my back. I had a feeling of dread but thankfully I managed to turn my body and my strength returned. I screamed for my Dad and we left the lights on all night until daylight.

CHAPTER 4

GRAVE YARD MIST
STORY BY CHAZZ LEE

I was taking a girl I met in work out on a date. We arranged to meet on a Saturday as we didn't work on weekends. I picked her up from her house at around 5pm. We didn't plan on where we going so we began to discuss where we should go as I drove along.

'I know where we can go,' she said, having a brain wave. 'There's a lovely place called The Windmill, it's in Ogmore-by-sea. The food there is lovely.'

I listened to her while she gave me directions on how to get to the place but it wasn't long before I realized that she didn't have a clue where she was going.

Bare in mind it was 1998 and no-one had sat navs back then. The best we could hope for was to ask someone for directions. But the road we were on was very lonely and surrounded by fields and mountains. What's more is was getting dark.

Somehow we ended up turning up a long narrow lane,

but the place it led us out to wasn't The Windmill, it was a graveyard with what looked to be a condemned church in the distance. The moonlit sky gave the place a creepy essence like something straight out of a horror movie.

The tombstones could just about be seen peeping over the mist that had appeared out of nowhere and which was very rapidly covering the whole area.

"The mist is heading straight for us!"

'What a creepy place,' I laughed. I was ready to scare her but the look on her face made me change my mind.

'Chazz… Look at the mist,' she whispered, looking straight ahead.

When I looked I saw the mist was now heading straight

for us. It moved from side to side as it edged its way forward like a living thing! I swear it was alive and was fully aware of what it was doing.

I didn't want to act scared in front of my date but natural instinct kicked in and I reversed the car at top speed until we were back on the main road. We ended up going somewhere else for food but our night had been ruined by the graveyard episode. No matter how I tried I just couldn't lighten the mood. We ended up going home early.

We didn't go out on another date but I'm glad to say we remained friends. A few weeks went by before she brought up what we'd seen at the graveyard.

'Chazz, I've been back to that place several times in the day and I can't find that graveyard anywhere.' I laughed and reminded her that she couldn't even find The Windmill pub let alone the whereabouts of that graveyard.

Out of curiosity I looked for the place myself, in the daylight of course. I've been back there over a dozen times and to this day I still can't find the place. If it did exist it doesn't exist any longer.

THE STRANGE MAN
STORY BY OPEY JOE

I was about eight years old and my brother Jim was six. We were with my dad in the scrap yard weighing in some metal. There were queues of lorries in front of us because something was wrong with the weighing scales. We were there for what seem like hours on a hot summer day.

My dad got out of the lorry and was having a chat with two men he knew who were parked in front of us. Me and Jim began to play games to pass the time away because we were bored stiff.

Five minutes hadn't gone by when we noticed a strange looking man with a buck mouth staring at us through the driver's window. He was stood a few feet away smiling at us. We were both terrified and we hid ourselves down. We slowly began to move back up to peep out and as we did the man was raising his head up through the window with us.

This happened several times, I swear it was as if he could see us through the door. He just kept smiling at us in a creepy fashion. He was bald with large ears that stuck out and his eyes looked evil.

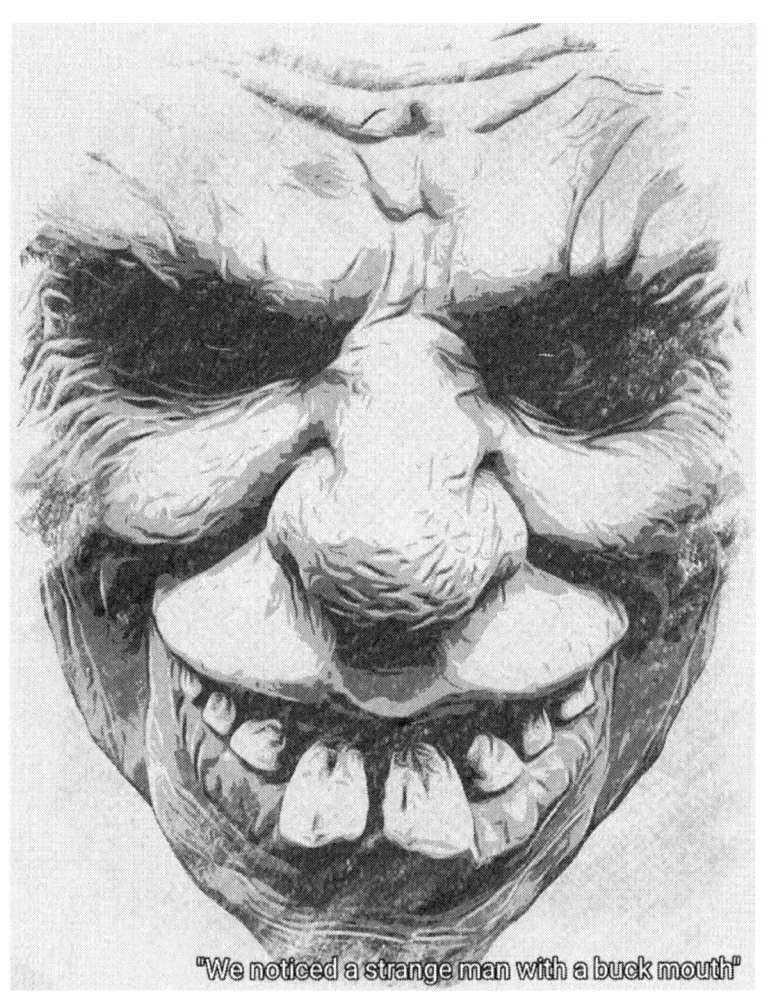

"We noticed a strange man with a buck mouth"

I know your probably thinking it could easily have been some loony playing games with us but my dad was literally ten feet from us and he was acting like he couldn't see him. Believe me if he had seen this man then he would have soon regretted it.

But I swear my dad couldn't see him. We began to scream for my dad and the strange man disappeared.

My dad came over to see what was the matter. We told him about the man and he had a quick look around. It's just your imagination he said getting back into the driver seat.

Thankfully we weren't there much longer as the scales were repaired. We returned to that scrap yard many times after but I never saw that strange man again. I don't think he was some kind of weirdo or a ghost for that matter, to be honest, my brother and I got the feeling that it was the devil himself. Don't ask me why but we both just knew it.

TUNNELS IN PYLE
STORY BY C. PROBERT

There are some old tunnels where I used to live in Pyle, Bridgend. I've never been afraid of the dark so I didn't care about going down there alone with just a torch light. The reason? I've always wanted to see a ghost.

I don't know why people are so afraid because for one thing they can't hurt you, two, they are only trapped spirits and three, if you are lucky enough to see one then it means that there's life after death.

One night I fell asleep on my bed while watching a movie. About 2am in the morning I was awoken by a strange yet calm voice.

'You know where to go,' it said.

Don't ask me why but I knew it meant the old tunnels. I got dressed and headed down there.

To get to the tunnels you had to go through some woods at the back of our campsite. Usually I'd have been excited by all of this but that night I have to admit I was a little freaked out. The hairs on the back of my neck stood up when I saw the tunnels up ahead.

I honestly felt like running all the way home but I took a deep breath, determined to conquer my fears.

I bent down to get into the tunnel and slowly made my way through. I was about half way down when I heard noises in front of me, like a group of people whispering. My breathing started to accelerate and my heart rate increased. I had a good torch beam however and could pretty much see everything in front of me.

The whispering sound increased before coming to a full stop as I neared the end of the tunnel. A frightening deep sound echoed out and a huge humanoid shadow appeared on the wall where my torch beam was pointed. It wasn't mine because my shadow was visible too. It was enough for me to turn around and run all the way home.

I jumped into my bed when I got into my caravan and covered the blankets over my head. I didn't remove them until daylight.

I don't know to whom the strange voice I heard that night belonged to and I don't know what was waiting for me at the end of that tunnel. One thing I learned though was that a ghost might not be able to hurt you but they can certainly give you heart failure if you were to see one.

NOISES ON THE ROOFTOPS AND THE GUARDIAN FAIRY
STORIES BY JULIA ROGERS AND S.S LEE

Julia's story
At first I thought it must be birds but then I realised it was too late at night. Maybe it was an owl or perhaps a bat. Whatever it was it was keeping me awake. Me and my husband Sam were on our summer travels in our caravan. We had settled onto some spare ground near to some woodlands in Pembrokeshire with our friends and family. The noise happened to wake my husband up too.

We both listened as, what sounded like tiny footsteps ran up and down the front of our caravan.

'Maybe it's a rat!' I said to my husband.

'The rat must be wearing boots,' he replied as we continued to listen.

Then we heard talking and giggling. We both knew this was no animal. We carried on listening, not really knowing what to think. We had quite a modern caravan with a large see-through skylight in the middle. I got up and was about to see if I could have a peep through the skylight when I saw I small evil face with two yellow eyes staring back at me.

Its long nose was pressed against the skylight and I could see it had a face shaped like a crescent moon with two pointed ears sticking out. I screamed for my husband to look and the little man ran away. My husband ran out with a broom and to his surprise everyone else was outside their caravans too.

They said that they'd heard footsteps on their roof for most of the night like we had. Footsteps and wicked laughter...

S.S Lees story
I was about ten years old when this happened. We lived on the same site in Evesham. My auntie's caravan was just across the road from ours and I'd visit her quite often.

One day I was running over to her plot when a small bright light flashed in front of me and stopped me in my tracks. 'Go back, go back,' it said before disappearing.

I heard my mam calling for me a moment later so I ran back home. Some boys on the site used to drive off really fast. I like to think the light I saw was a fairy protecting me.

DIVINE INTERVENTION
STORY BY GD JONES

We were living in Briton Ferry at the time and I was about fourteen years old. In case you didn't know Briton Ferry was a huge waste ground where lots of gypsy families settled. Obviously a place like that is bound to have its fair share of fly tippers, from the families who lived there and from people who lived somewhere else.

There were piles of rubbish everywhere. Household items, trees, stones and every other type of debris that you can imagine. Usually around 5pm, after tea, I'd be pretty bored, especially if my brothers or my friends were busy.

I'd get a kick out of setting fire to the trees that were dumped in every corner. Sometimes to add more fun I'd find a hairspray can to throw in for a big explosion.

Rummaging through some rubbish I couldn't believe my luck! I found a gas can, the ones you can buy to fill up lighters. My brothers Bill and Hope told me that they once put one of these cans into a fire and the entire place lit up. People even ran out of their caravans to see what had caused such an explosion. I rubbed my hands together and ran over to the pile of trees I'd just set fire to.

I stood back and threw the gas can right in the middle of them. I hid behind a huge rock and waited. And waited. And waited.

Five minutes had gone by and nothing had happened. I walked back over to the fire and I could see that the can had rolled off to the right, next to some branches that were not even lit. I got a stick and tried to roll the can back into the middle but as I poked at it, it went off!

The whole thing happened in slow motion. There was a big explosion and I could see nothing but flames all around me. I ran off believing I was on fire or my face was badly burnt.

There was a mirror on the floor amongst more tipped rubbish. I bent down in front of it to check my face. Nothing! Not a mark or a scratch. When I say that the flames were all around me I'm not exaggerating. But then I realized something. A few days previous I had found a prayer card in some rubbish. There was a picture of Mary and Jesus on the card and in the middle of them was a prayer that read: *Wherever I put myself, within thy sacred side and under the mental of our lady thy mother. Let thy holy angels stand about me and keep me in peace and let thy blessing be upon me. God bless our home amen.*

I'd been saying this prayer every morning since I'd found it. I believe the holy angels stood in front of the flames and protected me that evening. I told my mam about it and she believed they did too. I gave up lighting fires for fun from that day.

WET THE BED
STORY BY ANGELA CHAMBERS

I was staying over at my cousin's place for the weekend in Pembrokeshire. My uncle and auntie had a static caravan with three bedrooms inside. They are a big family so I had to share with my cousin who was also my best friend.

I arrived on the Saturday and after a day shopping and catching up with my friends and family by 8pm I was exhausted. My cousin Amy however did not feel the same. She was soon dressed and ready to hit the town. She begged me to go with her but I insisted she go with her sisters and her friends. She finally agreed after I promised her that we'd do something together the next day. After she'd gone, I went straight to bed.

At around 3am I heard someone come into the room. I assumed it was Amy so I didn't bother to look. She got into bed next to me. She felt wet and her breathing was heavy. I was so tired I didn't bother to look at her, I just thought she was drunk and had probably got caught in a heavy shower on her way home.

Next morning I woke up to an empty bed. I got dressed and walked into the living room where my auntie and uncle were sat.

'Morning, want a cup of coffee?' she asked, already making her way to the kitchen.

'Yes please,' I replied with a yawn. 'Where's Amy?' I asked.

'She stayed over a friend's house last night after one too many!' said my uncle.

'But she came into bed last night, she was soaked,' I said.

My auntie and uncle both looked at me shocked. 'Soaked? Was she breathing heavily?' asked my auntie, sitting next to me.

'Yes,' I replied.

'That wasn't our Amy,' replied my uncle. 'Many years ago, a young girl, walking home from a night out, fell into a river and drowned. Lots of people have been visited by her ghost. Exactly as you just described.'

SLEEP PARALYSIS
STORY BY ESTHER MAY

I've suffered with sleep paralysis for most of my life. Most of the time I just wake up and can't move, after a few seconds however, I manage to build up the strength to turn on my side and the frightening ordeal is over.

On one occasion though, it wasn't so easy. I was caring for my dad at the time and we were living in Salford in Manchester. After finishing my duties I went straight to bed. I woke up about 3am. I was completely paralyzed. I tried to cry out but I couldn't. I tried to turn on my side but I couldn't do that either. Usually these episodes last only a couple of seconds but this one had me gripped for over a minute.

There was an eerie feeling in the room like someone or something evil was with me. I began to say my prayers in my mind over and over and soon I was able to move my head from side to side. I'd kept my eyes closed because I was afraid to see what was in the room with me.

When I looked around I realized my nose was almost touching the ceiling! I was floating above my bed! Terrified I let out a scream and I came crashing down on my bed. My strength returned and I turned on all the lights. There's a lot of talk that the imagination runs away with you during a sleep paralysis. They say that the body is paralyzed while you sleep so that you don't act out your dreams and sometimes you wake up while the body is still paralyzed.

As a woman in her seventies I know from experience that this is not always the case. I have never had another episode of sleep paralysis like that one since and I hope I never do again.

MORE CASES OF SLEEP PARALYSIS
STORY BY BILLY AND JAMES

James's story
I went to sleep one night with rosary beads around my neck. I'd been suffering sleep paralysis more than usual so when my mam brought them home from church with her one day I gladly put them on.

I woke up about 2am paralyzed. Only this time it was different. I felt an evil presence next to me and it was choking me. Powerless to do anything else, I began to pray in my mind. I told whatever it was sitting next to me on my bed to go away. It began to loosen its grip and not only could I breathe I could move my body. I sat up and was ready to punch whatever it was tormenting me but nothing was there and so I felt as though I'd defeated the evil with my prayers and my rosary beads.

Next morning I woke up, my beads were missing from around my neck. I found them in pieces on the floor next to me.

Billy Doyle's story
Sleep paralysis runs in my family. I woke up one night unable to move. I could feel a horrible heat and there was an evil presence in my caravan. I didn't want to

open my eyes and look at what was there because I was too scared. I could feel something coming towards me but I had no voice to wake my wife sleeping next to me. I started to say my prayers because that's what usually works, but this time it didn't.

I could feel a presence on the bed, like whatever it was, was floating above me. I felt the blankets being tugged off me and I kept thinking it wants me to look at it. But I kept my eyes closed.

Then I heard a familiar voice saying, 'Bill it's me.' It was a departed family member who's name I won't mention in respect to the family. 'It's me, have a look,' it said, still tugging on the blankets.

I thought no way is this who it claims to be because of the evil feeling that came with it. I kept my eyes closed but it persisted. The voice grew more sinister and deep as it repeated itself over and over before growling at me.

I kept saying my prayers as it tugged at my blankets aggressively. Finally it went away and I was able to move my body again. I woke my wife straight after. She went back to sleep shortly after but I stayed up in fear that the evil presence would return. Thank God it never did.

STORIES MY DAD TOLD ME
STORY BY GD JONES

My mam had quite a few good ghost stories to tell me but so did my dad. One I remember was when he was a little boy. He and his brothers shared a tent together. They slept inside it mostly when my granddad and granny were traveling around with the horse and wagon.

One night he wandered quite a bit away from the tent to go to the toilet. While he was there relieving himself he said he saw a flash lightening in the sky and a fireball as big as a car landed on the ground not far from him.

The weird thing was it didn't explode it just landed safely on the ground. There was a strange humming sound coming from it. It lit up with a bight red colour every few seconds.

My dad was quite young and took off back to his brothers in the tent. When he went to show them the next morning it was gone!

Another story is from when he was about eighteen years old. Again he was traveling with his family, only this time he was sleeping by himself in his dad's lorry. They had settled in a place called Devils Bridge.

He said during the middle of the night that he saw a hideous red face with evil yellow eyes and two horns on its head grinning at him. It had no body, just a head. My dad resorted to violence and threw a punch at whatever it was grinning at him.

His hand went straight through it before it disappeared. He ran into the caravan where his brothers were sleeping and stayed there for the rest of the night. He told my granddad about it the following morning and he just laughed it off.

The very next morning my granddad seemed a bit uneasy as he told the boys to pack up because they were moving that day, despite his plans to stay there for at least two weeks.

A few days later he told my dad that he left the place so early because in the night he had seen the same hideous face staring at him through his window.

One of the other stories I remember him telling me and my brothers' was about an old man who predicted that when he died Swansea would shake. When he did die, just like he said, Swansea shook!

Another one was about a rich old woman called Loomy.

Supposedly she had sold her soul to the devil when she was younger for money. The devil warned her that when he came for her soul, her body would be found with her tongue hanging out.

One evening her daughter came to visit her and found her dead on the floor with a look of horror on her face and her tongue hanging out.

Another one he told us was about an old man named Peter Price who owned a farm. He was desperate for money and was in danger of losing his beloved farm. One night the devil came to him and offered him a fortune in return for his soul. Old Peter offered him a bargain. He told him he could have his soul if he could find one of his pigs that had a straight tail. But if he couldn't he got to keep the fortune put out in front of him.

The devil agreed and went out in search of a pig with a straight tail. But Peter knew pigs don't have straight tails, they have ringed ones. The devil never returned and he inherited a fortune.

The two last ones may have been made up to scare his six boys. But I had to share them because I think they're great.

HEAVENLY GUIDANCE
STORY BY A. B. JONES

My brother Pat was going to work in his new van. He'd got up late that morning and was going a bit faster on the roads than usual just to arrive on time. He was on the motorway speeding and overtaking cars.

All of a sudden from the back of his van he heard a voice saying, 'Slow down Pat.' He slowed down at once and drove carefully all the way to work. He believed that his Guardian angel was looking after him.

The same thing happened to my son Gwyn, aka GD Jones, the author of this book, and his dad. We'd just moved to south Wales and they were out in the van looking for scrap metal. At the same time they both heard a voice in the back saying, 'You are going the wrong way!'

They ignored the voice and they ended up turning off on a road they'd never been down before and got lost for about an hour before finding their way on the right road. My husband Yank said they had nearly ran out of petrol and just made it to a garage.

Another one happened to my mother and father. My

dad was a good time boy and he loved nothing better than a good drink up down the pub. My mam was always worried about him getting too drunk and falling over and hurting himself or worse, getting into a fight.

One night it was past closing time and the landlord was struggling to get my dad out of the pub. He phoned my mam up at home and told her that her husband was being a nuisance.

She arrived with my sister just in time as the barman had him by the coat and was ready to throw him out headfirst. They took hold of him but still he refused to leave and tried to get back in. The landlord was at his wits end and was ready to punch him. Still he refused to leave. My mother prayed for help and a few seconds later she saw my dad looking up at the sky.

A huge cloud had formed in the figure of what looked like Holy Mary. 'It's a sign from heaven for you to leave before the landlord loses his temper!' said my mother.

To their relief my dad agreed and blessed himself before staggering to their car. God only knows what might've happened if they hadn't seen that sign from heaven.

CHAPTER 5

BARKING UP THE WRONG TREE
STORY BY ERNIE HILL

There is an old story amongst travellers about a woman who gave birth to puppies. Supposedly she got a little passionate with her dog and well you know the rest. Now I don't know who this woman was but I've heard from different people who she might be and out of respect for her family I dare not say her real name so let's just call her Sandy.

Now the story goes that Sandy's offspring were the most hideous creatures imaginable. They were so ugly that the family put them all in a sack and threw them in a river to drown. All of them were thought to have died until years later when a rumour began to circulate that there had been sightings of a half-man / half-dog roaming around in Hackfall Wood, North Yorkshire.

Could it really be true that one of the woman's pups survived? As far as the stories go from the people who have encountered him roaming the woodlands, the Dogman is said to look identical to Benicio del Toro in the Wolfman movie. Only his fangs are much larger and his eyes are much more menacing.

Nobody as ever been hurt by him as far as I know but there were those who said that they'd been chased out of the woods by him after he came running at them barking and growling. The strange thing is, to my knowledge, he as never been seen by anyone else but people from the traveling community.

"I heard a growling noise"

Does he sense their presence as soon as they come into

his territory? And does he hold a grudge for being outcast by them?

I needed all these questions answering, so in 2014 I took a trip to Hackfall Wood. I walked around for most of the day equipped with a camera and a knife (should I need it) in search of the infamous Dogman. It was late in the evening when I decided to camp down for the night in my tent. I was exhausted from walking all day and I just needed a good rest.

I had a quality night vision camera, so if I were lucky enough to encounter the Dogman, I'd be ready!

Apart from the sound of birds and creatures in the undergrowth I heard nothing unusual. That was until about 12am. Something close by was walking through the trees. I could hear branches breaking under its feet as it came closer to my tent. I reached for my camera as I heard a strange growling noise, not like that of a dog but more like a person trying to impersonate one.

I thought that it might be a few of my friends who knew where I was going and had followed me to play pranks. Everything went quiet, then all at once my tent felt like it was being ripped apart!

There was no time to switch on my camera as I heard a terrifying hoarse voice say, 'GET OUT', in between ferocious barks, which sounded like an angry Rottweiler!

Then silence. I was shaking uncontrollably as I reached for my camera. I turned it on and peeped outside. Nothing! If indeed this was the Dogman he had now gone. To be honest I was petrified he would come back and kill me if I didn't leave at that moment. I left everything behind accept from my knife and camera. If I was to encounter him again on my way home I'd be sure to get a shot of him.

I made it back to my van without incident. I took one look at the woods before I left. If I'd not left those woods that night, I do believe that I wouldn't have made it out alive. The Dogman gave me one warning and one warning only. I was lucky to see his human side, I dread to think what would've happened if I was to witness his beast side.

Of course I've told many people about my story but not many believe me. Maybe you should take a trip down to Hackfall Wood and see for yourselves.

THE FACE IN THE PARK AND THE EVIL VOICE
STORY BY BILL JONES

"it kept staring and smiling at me"

I was playing hide and seek with my dad, my brothers and sister in a park in Accrington. We all went our separate ways to find a good hiding spot while my brother Hope counted to twenty with his hands covering his face. One by one we were found until it was only my dad who was missing. Usually he was easy to find but this time, we couldn't find him anywhere.

We all went in search of him. I headed towards a patch of lumpy grass because I thought I saw a face peeping out from behind it. I presumed it was my dad and I shouted to the others that I'd found him.

There was some people walking their dog and they'd heard us calling for our dad. 'Are you looking for your dad?' they said. 'He's up yonder behind the wall!' they said before heading off.

'No he's here,' I said, heading for the patch of lumpy grass.

As I got closer the face peeked out at me again. I could see it wasn't my dad at all. It was bald with dark skin and an evil complexion. If anyone as ever seen the monster from the Jeepers Creepers movie, that's how I can best describe it. It kept staring at me and smiling.

My dad came out from behind an old stone wall a few hundred yards away. He saw me heading towards the patch of lumpy grass where the evil face seemed to be all the more pleased as I came closer to it. He told us all to run, he seemed to be panicking a little. I turned away from the face and ran over to my dad with my brothers and sister.

On the way home he told us that he hadn't planned on coming out of his hiding spot until he saw a cloud shaped like Holy Mary in the sky. I couldn't help but think what would have happened if my dad hadn't seen Mary in the sky, appearing to give us some sort of warning. Maybe the face I'd seen hiding behind the patch of lumpy grass belonged to the devil.

WARM BY THE FIRE
STORY BY ANN WILLIAMS

When I was a child, I had a fever. I was really ill and my dad sat up with me all night. It was the middle of winter and it was freezing in our caravan. The wind was blowing and the rain was coming down heavy.

We had run empty on coal for the fire stove and I was starting to get chills. My dad had put a damp towel on my head to keep my temperature down. I looked over to the kitchen and saw that there was an old woman sitting in a chair looking at me.

I was scared of her at first until she got up and lit a glorious fire for us. She looked familiar as she smiled at me before disappearing. The fire lasted all night and I was better in the morning. I thought my fever had made me hallucinate the whole thing until my dad said that he'd seen the exact same thing before I even mentioned it to him.

He believed that the old woman must've been his mam sent from heaven to look after us.

CREEPY OLD WOMAN
STORY BY REBECCA LEWIS

When I was about ten years old me and my sister shared a bunk bed. My oldest sister would sleep at the top and I would sleep at the bottom. One night I was alone in my room. I was laying in my bed drifting off, when I saw a creepy old woman standing in the room. She wasn't transparent, I could literally see every detail of her clothes. Neither was she looking at me, she was just staring at the wall. I kept watching her standing there motionless until I fell asleep.

I told my sister about it the next morning but she fobbed it off as just my imagination. I began to believe that she was right until a few nights later, I was alone in my room again when all my sisters books began to fall off the shelf one after another. I ran out of my room screaming. Nothing strange happened again after that night, but I made sure I was never alone in my room again.

BOING SOUND
STORY BY GD JONES

Me and my brother were throwing some rubbish over a fence at the bottom of our site late at night. We were nearly finished when we heard a strange bong sound. There was a busy main road by the entrance of our site and the strange sound literally went past us, like a wheel bouncing along the road. Strange thing was we could hear it but we couldn't see anything. We both jumped inside the van and took off.

A day or two later we told our friend about what we'd heard. We had only just moved to the site but our friend had been living there for over five years. We were shocked when he told us that years before, there had been a car accident in the bus stop near the entrance of our site. Two little girls had been killed while waiting for a bus and one of the tyres of the car that killed them had come off during the crash and had bounced right the way down the road. Apparently the campsite was said to be so haunted at one time, that the Carol family who had lived there for years brought a priest down to bless the entire place.

THE GOBLIN MAN
STORY BY CARL LOCKE

This is not much of a ghost story but when I first got married I woke up in the middle of the night with what looked to be a goblin with his little hands around my neck, trying to strangle me. I couldn't see his face, just his dark shadowy figure. I fought him off and he disappeared into the dark. I was wide-awake when it happened and me and my wife stayed up all night afterwards with the lights and TV on so it was definitely not a bad dream.

The reason I wanted to share this story is because GD Jones and his brother Bill had a similar experience.

THE FATHER, SON AND THE HOLY SPIRIT
STORY BY OPEY JONES

I always questioned the holy trinity. How could there be three gods in one? Me and my mam and brother used to argue about it. They'd give me good answers when I would question them about it but still I couldn't believe it.

I was in church one evening with my two boys. I watched as the priest changed the bread and wine into the body and blood of Christ. I couldn't believe my eyes. I saw as clear as daylight a beautiful white dove flying into the golden chalices where the bread and wine is placed and poured into.

I still don't fully understand the Holy Trinity as I'm sure many of you don't. But I think I got a sign from heaven telling me to stop questioning and just believe.

A SCREAMING SOUND
STORY BY WILLIAM DOYLE

I was playing snakes and ladders with my brothers one evening by the fire stove in our caravan. In the middle of the game we heard a high-pitched screaming sound. My parents thought it might be someone outside playing tricks but further investigation led them to a rubbish bag inside our caravan. My dad picked the bag up from the floor and looked inside. He seemed shocked by what he saw. He ran outside with the bag and threw it over the wall.

He said that there was just something inside the bag that got to close to the fire and made a squeaking sound as it melted. It seemed like just a cover up and he would never tell us what was really in the bag no matter how many times we asked.

I remember we threw a creepy action figure toy in the same rubbish bag a few days before. It used to freak me and my brothers out because it would seem to put itself in a different position from the one you left it in every time you turned away from it. If you stood it up, it would sit itself down. If you sat it down and turned away from it, you'd find it standing back up. I guess our suspicions were right. It did have a mind of it's own after all.

MY VISIT TO KILGETTY
STORY BY GD JONES

I drove up to Kilgetty to visit my old friend Chazz Lee. He

invited me to come up because he promised me that, not only did he have a few more ghost stories to tell me but so did his wife Barbara. I was coming towards the end of this book and I really didn't want to go any further than 'Chapter 5' so I decided to put all of their tales together in one story.

CHAZZ'S STORY

Me and my friend Bill were walking his dogs through a cornfield in Cae Garw farm where I used to live. The corn had grown quite high, about six feet tall, so it was hard to see where you were going once you got in the middle of it. It was dusk when we set off and by the time we were on our way home it had gone dark.

We had our torches with us and were messing about switching them off and on to scare each other. The last time I switched mine off was when I heard something running through the corn stalks at the side of us.

I switched it back on and pointed it in the direction that I'd heard the noise but the corn was so thick it was hard to see. I pointed back down the path we'd made on our way through when we'd left and I swear I saw a small creature peeping at us up ahead. I told Bill that I thought I saw something but he laughed it off, believing I was trying to scare him.

All the way home I could hear something running through the corn stalks behind us, every now and then I'd flash my torch behind us and see the same little creature peeping at us, each time it was getting closer and closer. Its body was full of green spikes and its eyes were big and white. Thankfully I could see the streetlights of our campsite up ahead. I flashed my torch beam behind me once again and saw the creature standing behind us in full view no more than fifteen feet away.

It looked like it had lots of hair covering its body with two large ears sticking up from its troll-like face. I ran as it came running towards us. Bill, who still thought it was all a joke, kept up with me and before we knew it we were back in the safety of our campsite. I flashed my torch beam back into the cornfield but couldn't see anything.

Although the dogs began to bark at something that we couldn't see. I told him what I'd seen in there and he asked me to go back in to find the creature. He even suggested we set the dogs loose on it.

I said no way and I went home and never returned to

that field until all the corn was cleared. I have no idea whether it was a fairy or an alien creature but it seemed happy to dwell inside the cornfields.

THE LITTLE GIRL IN RAGGED CLOTHES

My mam and my sister Amanda have both seen a little girl dressed in ragged clothes playing outside their caravan. They say she always hides behind the shrubs in her garden when she sees them looking and peeps at them from behind the bushes. They say she has blonde hair tied in pigtails and wears a dirty ripped old-fashioned dress. They aren't scared of her, in fact, they feel sorry for her because something bad must have happened in her life and her spirit remains trapped in this world.

I don't know if this has something to do with the little girl but one night when I was visiting my mam, we heard a knock on the door. My natural response was to say come in, but nobody did, I went to open the door but nobody was there. I sat back down and my mam said, 'Didn't you see that shadow of a little boy come in and walk out?'

'No,' I said.

'You shouldn't say come in without seeing who was there!' said my mam.

'Why not?'

'Because you don't know who you're inviting in!' said my mam.

I didn't think much more of it and went to sleep on the settee. Later that night, I was awoken by someone covering me over with the blankets. I heard them walking about in my mother's static caravan before I fell back to sleep.

Next morning I thanked my mam for covering me over during the night.

'What are you talking about boy? I never got up last night!'

There was only me and my mam at home and I'm a certain I wasn't dreaming. Maybe it was the shadow of the little boy or the little girl in ragged clothes? Maybe it was both!

BARBARA'S STORY

We have seen and heard many strange things in the yard were we live in Kilgetty. Little boys and girls dressed in old-fashioned clothing, walking past both our caravan and my parents, before disappearing into thin air. Noises of trains going past when there are no train tracks for miles.

Both me and my husband Chazz heard a church bell gong several times, when there are no churches in the small village where we live. Ironically the day after we heard this, Chazz's father sadly past away. What's even more strange is that, exactly one year from the day he past away, at exactly the same time we first got the news, Chazz heard the church bell gong again several times.

My parents have seen many strange things here too. My dad put up CCTV cameras all around the yard and one of the strangest things he captured was a white mist floating around the yard and flying back and forth to the camera.

Late, almost every night, if you listen closely, you can hear the sound of people whispering and weird laughter from inside the woods next to us.

One day a woman came to our place. She'd heard about it being haunted so she was taking pictures on her phone hoping to capture something out of the ordinary. When she looked at her pictures she was surprised to see an old man standing by our fence and also the shadowy figure of a nun on the wall further up.

Chazz has also captured some strange phenomena on his camera phone, one of which he showed to GD Jones when he came to visit us. When my husband showed him the photo, they both agreed that what he captured looked like a ghostly red dragon. My parents were just having the final touches done to their static caravan. The dragon's head can be seen on the floor a few feet away from the caravan with its long tail poking out from the other end.

Up the road from where we live, there is an old antique shop. I saw a weird looking statue of a witch for sale in there one morning. I bought it and took it home. My husband didn't like the look of it as soon as he saw it, but I liked it and put it on display inside our living room.

A few days went by when the mother of the woman I bought it from came down to visit us with her husband, who just happened to be the vicar who married me and Chazz.

'Has the witch talked to you yet?' she asked.

'No!' I replied.

'Didn't my daughter tell you that it's haunted?' she smiled.

After they left my husband made me take it out of the caravan. He wants me to get rid of it but I want to keep it. Not only has it got a certain charm about it, it's also good to scare our guests at Halloween.

Throughout my life I've had many paranormal experiences. One of the most creepy was when me and my friend were driving home from a visit to my aunts in Pembrokeshire. It was dark and up ahead we could see a man on a bike. My friend hesitated before overtaking him.

When we did we could see he was dressed in old-fashioned clothing and his bicycle looked like it was from early 1900s. We looked back in the wing mirror as we past him and he'd vanished!

Little did we know the area we were driving along was notorious for ghostly sightings of several nuns riding on bicycles and a group of mourners following a funeral car.

On another occasion, me and Chazz had picked up some chairs and tables from his father, who was doing boot sales almost every Saturday and Sunday. We thought we'd try our hand at it to earn some extra cash. One of the items his father gave us was an old invalid chair from a hospital. We loaded it in the back of our van with some other stuff. Halfway home, we heard someone talking in the back. We both had a feeling the invalid chair was haunted so we pulled the van to one side and threw it out at the side of the road.

I am fascinated with the paranormal and occasionally I attend a ghost hunt inside an old castle, twenty miles from where we live.

The only experience I've had so far was when we walked into one of the rooms. I saw a dark shadow that looked darker than night flying around the ceiling.

When me and Chazz were first married, we lived on a campsite in Whitland. We'd heard about people seeing the ghost of a man who'd been killed crossing the railway lines. People who'd seen his ghost said that you could see his decapitated body searching around for his head. I never saw this headless ghost but late one night I could hear the sound of someone crying. I peeped out the window and saw a white ghostly figure hovering along the road of our campsite. Whether or not it was connected to the headless man I do not know.

ANOTHER STORY FROM CHAZZ

My sister and brother were coming home from visiting family with my mam and dad. They were driving along a dark road in Ross-on-Wye. As they were driving along my sister and brother noticed a woman standing at the side of road with her head hung down. They thought it strange for someone to be standing all alone outside so late with the nearest town or village miles away in either direction. She lifted her head as they past her and they both saw that it was an old woman with her eyes and nose missing from her wrinkled glowing face.

I guess it could've been someone wearing a mask and standing at the side of the road to play a prank on passing cars, but the weird thing about it was, my brother and sister were the only ones who saw her standing there at the side of the road. We later heard that the old woman has been sighted at that very same spot on numerous occasions at that time of night by many people. She is believed to be the wife of a farmer. The story goes that he had caught her cheating with one of the workers and shot her in the face.

PERSONAL NOTE FROM G D JONES

Me, Chazz and his wife Barbara talked for ages about their ghostly experiences. I was more than pleased with the stories they gave me for my book. An eerie thing happened to me after I left their place and was on my way home. It was cold and the windows began to steam up. That's when I began to notice creepy drawings appearing on my windscreen. Matchstick men with horns and angry faces. Some had two heads with tails. It couldn't have been Chazz or his wife and kids playing tricks because I would've noticed. My car was parked right outside their home and was clearly visible from the window. It was getting dark so I parked up and wiped off the drawings from my window.

STRANGE DREAMS
STORY BY GD JONES

I've had many strange dreams but the weirdest three I've ever had were not like dreams at all. In fact they seemed so real that I woke up screaming. I've had some funny ones too, like when I dreamt my brother Jim was trying to sell a motor to some men. While he was showing them around one of them hit him behind the head. I was watching from the bottom of the campsite and quickly ran up to help him. I grabbed one in a headlock and started to punch him.

I woke up holding my pillow in a tight grip and was punching it for all I was worth.

Others I've had were not so funny, like a giant T-Rex roaming around our campsite while everyone was hiding. Or getting caught in a huge spider web and having my blood drained out of me by a big spider, after it sank its fangs into my neck. I woke up screaming with that one and scared the life out of my brother Tom who was sleeping in the same trailer as me.

I think there's more to dreams than meet the eye. After all, the content and purpose of them are still not fully understood by science. There are plenty of stories out there by people claiming to have been visited in their dream by a departed family member to either give them a message or to let them know they're alright. There are some people who claim to have had premonitions in their dreams. My mam often had dreams about a plane crashing. The dream would always be different but it would always end with a plane crashing. She predicted that one day something bad would happen involving a plane. She had this dream quite often over the space of over fifteen years, from when we lived in Salford right up to when we were living in Pyle, Bridgend.

One afternoon on September 11th 2001 we saw on the news that planes had crashed into the World Trade Center. This is my dream she said. I told you something bad was going to happen one day. She never had the dream again after that day.

My brother Hope dreamt that he was queuing in a long line to get to heaven. At the top of the queue there was a man letting people through the gates into paradise. Behind him though lurked a horrible little creature pacing back and forth. In the background behind it there was a dried up desert land with starving animals and carcasses sticking out of the ground. He believed that this dream was a vision of heaven and hell.

One night not long after my parents got married, the two of them woke up in a cold sweat about 2am. They told each other about their nightmare and they realized that they'd both had the exactly the same dream, that they were both being strangled in chains. How is it possible that two people can share the same dream?

I'd like to share two strange dreams I had with you that are both scary and downright disturbing…

THE WEIRDEST NIGHT OF MY LIFE

It was New Years Eve 2007. I had bad toothache all through the day from all the chocolate and sweets I'd eaten all over Christmas. Shops were closed early that evening because of the holidays so I walked to the other side of the campsite were my brother lived. I knocked on his caravan door and asked if he or his wife had any painkillers for me. Unfortunately they didn't so I headed back home.

My friend Jumbob who lived a few plots down from where my brother's place was saw me walking away in agony. He asked me what was wrong. After I told him all about my rotten tooth he said that he had very strong *Co-codamol* tablets that would help.

I took two of them as soon as I got home. My dad was in hospital at the time and my mam always went to bed by 7pm after a few glasses of wine. Thankfully the pain began to wear off but I was exhausted after being up in pain for most of the previous night. It was around 8pm when I decided to call it a night.

I woke up God knows what time to the sound of a helicopter. I could literally feel my caravan shake as it seemed to draw nearer. I uncovered the blankets from myself and couldn't believe my eyes. There was a green helicopter inside my caravan with two pilots inside. I pulled the blankets back over me as it headed straight towards me.

Everything went silent. I peeped from underneath my blankets and was relieved that the green helicopter was gone. However, now there was a purple shadow peeping at me from my doorway. I threw a shoe at it and told it to piss off! I tried to go back to sleep but a chorus of voices began to tell me not to go back to sleep or I wouldn't wake up. I'd had enough! I grabbed my blankets and pillow and stormed out of my caravan and headed for my parent's one.

When I got outside and reached for the door handle however, it seemed to go further and further from my reach. Somewhere close by I could hear Jimbob laughing hysterically as I tried in vain to reach for the door handle of my parent's caravan.

I woke up in my dad's bed, God knows how I got there. My toothache was gone but my head was spinning. Whatever was in those pills he gave me last night? I thought. Was it all a dream or a hallucination?

I told everyone about my strange experience and they all

found it very funny. Jumbob swore that there was nothing wrong with the tablets and that he strongly advised me not to drink alcohol before taking them. I didn't drink alcohol, so if it wasn't the painkillers that brought it on then what on earth did?

THE VISITOR

I was on my way to Maesteg. The woman I'd worked for that day told me to call back in the evening so she could pay me. The road to Maesteg is very dark and lonely with not a street light for miles.

I was looking at the stars as I drove along. I remember thinking how spectacular they looked without any streetlights around.

I noticed two of them moving. One was moving from side to side and the other one was going around it in circular motions. How odd! I thought to myself. I kept on watching until they merged together in a straight line before disappearing. This scared the life out of me. I'd seen the movie 'Fire in the Sky' where Travis Walton got abducted for five days and I didn't plan on experiencing it myself. I turned the van around and headed home as fast as I could go.

That same night I had the strangest dream I've ever had. I've written a science fiction novel, 'The Future Assassin' and a collection of stories, 'Theory Tales' and if I really wanted to, I could write another one inspired by this dream.

Maybe I dreamed it because I was scared of the UFOs I'd seen or maybe it was because my mind was still in overdrive because of the books I was writing or maybe I'd just been reading too many Stephen King books, whatever the reason it seemed so real. Like I was really there and it was actually happening to me.

I was driving home from work and the snow was coming down heavy. I took a short cut home through the lanes as I always do when driving home from Maesteg. I was driving slowly because of the awful weather and was finding it difficult to see out of the window even though I had the windscreen wipers on full speed.

A car came fast from around a bend. I had no time to react. My wheels skidded and glass shattered as our two vehicles collided.

I woke up to unfamiliar surroundings. I was laying in bed with my leg in a cast. The small room I found myself in was pleasantly decorated. There was a TV in the corner and my bed was right now next to a window. I could see that it was still snowing heavily outside. As I lay there, taking in my surroundings the door of my room opened up and in walked a young woman.

She was the image of Katie Melua and I thought at last my luck had come in. 'You're awake,' she said with a smile as she sat next to me on the bed.

'Am I in hospital?' I asked.

'No I managed to get you out the wreckage and bring you to my house. We had a nasty accident back there, thank goodness you got away with just a broken leg.'

'Was it you I crashed into?'

'Yes,' she replied a little prudently. 'We'll have to phone our insurance companies to sort it out once you're fit and ready. Let's not worry about that now though, the main thing is to get you better! Unfortunately the snow as disrupted everything, the phone lines are down and I have no signal on my smartphone. Once they are up and running again I'll call for an ambulance.'

She seemed kind and gentle. I couldn't have cared less if the phone lines were down forever. I was already infatuated with this woman and by the way she was acting and looking at me, I got the feeling that she felt the same way about me. I told her she looked like Katie Melua and she laughed shyly and told me that her name was actually Kate.

For the next couple of days she attended to my every need, not just like a nurse but like an angel as well. She'd pull up a chair by my bed and we'd watch TV and have dinner together. We'd talk for hours about all the things we liked and enjoyed in life. We had so much in common that it seemed impossible. But she'd always go missing for hours too. I guessed she had lots of other things to do apart from look after me.

When she returned to my room, I told her that I hoped my leg would never heal and the snow would last forever so that I could stay with her. She smiled and kissed me on the lips before leaving me again. Night-time came and I couldn't stop smiling as I drifted off to sleep.

Then I awoke with a start. I could hear someone screaming in pain from close by. I sat up in my bed and listened. The screams sounded like they were coming from a man. I called for Kate over and over but she didn't respond. I had to see what was happening. I slid off my bed and managed to make it to the door. It wasn't locked and when I opened it and left my room I found myself standing in a long corridor.

There were lots of other doors each side as I limped along following the noise. I was soon standing in front of a green door and the screaming noise was coming from inside this room. I took a deep breath before I pushed it open. I saw a man laying in bed in a room identical to mine. He had the bed sheets up, covering his obese body. He looked surprised when he saw me limping over to his bed.

I assumed he was paralyzed as he could only move his head from side to side. 'Help me,' he said desperately. 'You must help me before she comes back to finish me off!'

'Who are you talking about?' I asked, sitting next to him on the bed.

'That thing is not what she seems, she appears in the form of whatever your heart desires... to fool you!'

'She's doesn't care about us! She's only here to feast on us! Help me out of here before she comes back.'

'Where has she gone?' I asked.

'Probably to find more like us. That's why she has all those rooms - to store them up!' The man begged me to help him again so I uncovered the sheets to lift him out of bed and was horrified by what I saw. His arms and legs were missing! Blood was dripping from what was left of his limbs like they'd been pulled off! I ran out of the room in a panic.

It couldn't be true! Surely this was not the work of the kind beautiful woman I'd come to know as Kate. There was a mirror on the wall and I could see how much weight I'd put on, over fifty pounds at least. As I limped down the corridor I began to open the door of every room I passed. In each bed I saw the remains of a human body laying inside. I was about to open the door to my own room when I heard Kate calling my name.

'I see your able to walk again,' she smiled, only this time her smile wasn't the same. Her mouth seemed bigger and her teeth looked sharp and rotten. Her eyes weren't the same either. They were red and evil.

'Keep away from me,' I said, as she walked closer to me with what looked like a hunch in her back.

'Has someone told you my secret?'

She looked down at the floor before looking back to me menacingly. 'Well then, I've had my dinner… now it's time for dessert!'

At that moment she changed into her true terrifying form. I ran limping into my room and shoved a chair against the door handle so she couldn't get in. I headed for the window but I couldn't lift it open.

The door of my room was soon ripped opened and there stood the hideous green monster, ready to bite my head off with its razor sharp teeth. I picked up another chair and threw it at the window. The winter scenery outside split in two like a painting being torn in half. In it's place I could see stars outside and the Earth itself. Before I had time to realize that this was not a house at all but an alien spacecraft in disguise, I was sucked out of there like a vacuum. I could hear the monster laughing as I fought for my breath and floated further and further out into space…

I woke up in a cold sweat breathing heavy but gratefully. It all seemed so real. People laugh whenever I tell them about my dream or nightmare. To them it's just my overactive imagination going into overdrive while I sleep. But the most weird part of all this is, since I saw those UFOs that evening, I have that dream all of the time.

Maybe now that I've shared it with all of you, it will haunt someone else's dreams instead of mine.

The End

CONCLUSION

A ghost sighting or a strange paranormal event might not always be what they seem. That's what I've always believed. In my first book, **The Future Assassin**, I wrote about a freak of nature in certain places around the world causing one era of time to meet with another, which I like to call a time clash. Whatever time line you are standing on, past, present or future, you believe the other person your seeing in their time line to be a ghost.

In one of the short stories in my second book, **Theory Tales**, I mention the Earth itself, possibly being a living organism, able to remember events in history and allowing us to witness them as a sort of mirage.

I do have one last theory to leave you with however before we bring this book to an end. What if everything we do and say on Earth is being recorded, monitored and watched? What if sometimes these, possibly, holographic recordings of our past are played out to us purposely or accidentally by a higher intelligence from another world or even by God almighty himself from heaven?

The scientist in me is always trying to come up with a rational explanation of what a ghost or paranormal experience might be whenever I hear one.

Then again, maybe there is no rational explanation that's what keeps us intrigued with tales of the paranormal.

Published by
www.publishandprint.co.uk

If you enjoyed this book then please leave a positive review on Amazon and also check out G. D. Jones other books.

Printed in Great Britain
by Amazon